A Crown Worth Fighting For

Stephanie Basco Sullivan

A Crown Worth Fighting For

Cover photo by Shane Sullivan

ISBN 10: 1-888141-18-2
ISBN 13: 978-1-888141-18-4

Published by:
Southeast Media Productions
Carlisle, Pennsylvania
U.S.A.
Semediapro.com

Foreword

E vents in history are brimming with endless "what ifs." The Tudor dynasty has always captured my attention, especially during the time of Henry VIII's reign. From his splendid coronation in 1509, at the age of seventeen, to his death in 1547 when he was just fifty-five years old, Henry left a legacy behind him that is still talked about and debated to this day. But what he is most known for are his six wives and how quickly he went through them.

Someone recently asked the question, *what would have happened if Henry had died after his jousting accident in 1536?* He was married to Anne Boleyn, his second wife. Catherine of Aragon had passed away, and both queens had given him a daughter each. He did have a bastard son by his former mistress, Bessie Blount, but only recognized him when he realized his first wife could no longer bear him children. Henry's new wife and queen, Anne Boleyn, had just suffered a miscarriage but found herself with child shortly after. While all of Henry's hopes rested on the child she carried, he had secretly started planning his next marriage just in case Anne lost the child or failed in her promise of a son and heir. Regardless of the circumstances, if the mighty King of England had died in 1536 leaving his pregnant wife— and very young daughter, Elizabeth—at the mercy of the English people, what might have happened? Would history have been altered so much so that Henry would have been practically erased from English history, or would his legacy have lived on through his daughters, Mary and Elizabeth?

With these thoughts in mind, I felt a challenge to open my mind and truly put myself in Anne Boleyn's shoes. Try to see the world through her eyes. After all, she was only human, and I have no doubt that if she had survived Henry's wrath in his pursuit of a prince, I believe Tudor history would have been reduced to a footnote. So clear your mind of everything you know about good ole Henry VIII, and open your eyes to a world where there never was the famous saying, "Divorced, beheaded, died, divorced, beheaded, survived."

Remember, this book is a work of fiction, based on some facts. I hope all Tudor enthusiasts will enjoy a different point of view.

TABLE OF CONTENTS

"The Most Happy"   Queen Anne Boleyn 1533-1536

Chapter One

"**O**h, my dearest one, I have eyes for no other. You have captured my soul with your captivating gaze, and now my heart belongs to you." Henry's voice could be heard so closely that she swore he was inside her ear. But when she turned to caress his handsome face with her touch and kiss his hungry lips, he was not there. "Henry, my love, where ever have you gone? Stop playing on my emotions, and give me true love's kiss." But all she could see was the darkness that surrounded her, and the sound of her voice echoed off the emptiness that covered her like a blanket.

Where am I? Where is Henry? I can hear his voice but I cannot find him. A glimmer of light caught her attention. She turned to face the direction it came from only to find that her hand already rested on the door. "My own darling, the reason for my burning desires, I love only you. Come to me so that I may free my mind of this cruel torture of not getting to hold you in my arms." *Here I am my love, my husband; I shall cool your passions.* Before she had the door pushed open, she realized that she was not the one Henry was talking to—it was the Lady Jane Seymour.

"Henry, how could you? I am your beloved, your true and loyal wife. It is your son I now carry." But neither Henry nor Jane seemed to see or hear her. Maybe if I slap his face or shove his affections off his lap, they would notice me here. Walking over to the lover's scene unfolding in front of her, Henry kissed Jane on the neck. In return, Jane placed her affections on Henry's lips. "Oh, sweet Jane, your lips have quenched my thirst like no other. I had not thought that your kiss would calm my heart's ache, like kissing your neck had done, but it has, and now I can truly call you mine." Anne's hands reached out to grab the thin and pale Lady Jane, but her hands seemed to disappear when they came in contact with the elusive figure, leaving her feeling beyond confused.

"Once we are married, my love. I dare not damage your reputation. You are by nature a true lady and queen. I want nothing to distort or blemish your sweet and honest demeanor. I want nothing to be given or revealed to me just now. Ten days from now, I shall bathe myself in your pureness and piety. You must think of your motto. All queens have one, and I have no doubt that through my love, you will have one that upholds everything that is good within you." *His queen! Henry, what are you talking about? I am your queen, I'm still here. Have you gone extremely mad?* Was there no end to this nightmare? The light that had illuminated her worst dream grew dim, and Henry, along with Jane, gradually disappeared as slowly as they had emerged. She could feel her heart skip a beat as she lost sight of her husband. Just when she thought that maybe her eyes would open to awaken her, she heard soft cries coming from another dark corner in her dreamed world. She turned in the direction from which the sadness beckoned her. As she approached, she saw three women standing around a wooden box. She could not make out their faces, but it was obvious that they were beside themselves with grief. As she seemed to glide closer to see what—or who—was in the box, something stopped her from getting too close. Whatever had its grip on her appeared determined not to let her see whom the women were crying for. One of the shadowed figures whispered, "My poor queen. Death was not fair in poisoning the king to take her life, especially when there was a young child to consider."

Oh, sweet Lord, is that me? Is this the only farewell I receive after my death? And why did she say the king took my life? Death, if this is your prediction, please wake me now, so I may see my daughter one more time. I carry yet another life inside of me that may very well be a prince and heir for His Majesty. She glanced in the direction of the grieving women, and just like jumping into a pond during winter, Anne jolted awake, away from her disturbing nightmare.

Anne sat straight up in bed, pulling in a huge gulp of air to fill her aching lungs. Beads of sweat ran down her face and neck, stopping where her cotton night gown began. Even though it was January and snow covered most of the ground, the horrible dream she found herself rousing from could have melted everything until spring showed up. The fire that lit her bedchamber crackled and popped as if it were feeling her anxieties. "Nan, fetch me some cool water, please." She felt like she could have drained the Thames, and she would still feel depleted of all life's moisture.

"Is everything all right, Your Grace?" Nan asked sincerely, handing Anne a silver chalice filled with the requested water. "Yes, Nan, everything is well. I just had a bad dream." The cool water felt so good to her dry tongue that she quickly asked for another.

"Nan, what time is it? With the curtains drawn and the shutters closed, it's hard to tell anymore." Anne tried to squint through the slivers of wood that adorned her windows, but whether it was still dark, or that she was not awake enough, she could not tell by her own accord.

"It is just before six, Madam; the sun has just begun to rise. I do believe it will be a most beautiful day for the jousting tournaments, despite snow still being on the ground." Nan had started pulling back the heavy, dark curtains that enclosed her bed, while another lady began opening the wooden slats so that the sunlight could make its grand entrance. The sun was a much-welcomed addition to the stifling atmosphere that had been dredged up through her nightmare.

"Would you please ask for my sister, Mary, to attend me this morning? Please have enough meat and bread brought up for two, and tell her to dress for mass." Anne reached for the dressing gown that had been laid out for her. She pulled the green velvet coverlet over her sweat-soaked nightgown and quickly fastened it so no one could see it. A pitcher of fresh water had been brought up for her to rinse her face and hands. Since the winter season was still in full swing, there were no fresh-cut flowers at her disposal to add fragrance to her water. Luckily, Nan had made sure to stock up on scented oils from the market when the first winds of winter had begun to blow.

Anne opened a tiny vial labeled *lavender with rose petal*. She poured a little of the oil into the water basin. The calming and fresh scent instantly filled her bedchamber. She placed a piece of linen cloth in the cool water, allowing it to soak up the soothing aromas. After ringing the excess water from the cloth, she began washing her face and neck, stopping when she brought the cloth to her mouth and nose. She inhaled deeply. Her entire body seemed to absorb the calming and fresh aroma that the oil provided. She proceeded to wipe down her arms and hands. The quick rinsing did great wonders in bringing her back to reality. Someone else must have enjoyed the beautiful and soothing scent, as well, because just as she placed the cloth on the rack to dry, Anne felt the quickening inside her womb spring to life.

"Good morning, sweet prince," she said softly as she smiled, cradling her slightly swollen belly. "I trust you rested better than your mother did? Have no worries, it was merely a dream—that's all." To give them both reassurance, she gently patted her belly and quickly thought about happy things, like having a much-deserved breakfast before morning mass, the fact that it was, indeed, a most beautiful day. Just as she approached the front parlor of her chambers, a door opened. It was her sister, Mary. Anne was always happy to see her siblings. Even though Mary had attracted the attentions of Anne's husband long before Anne became queen, Anne had always been close to her siblings, especially Mary. Indeed, they were all very close, confiding in one another as if they were in confession. "Mary, good morning, dear sister, please join me and your future king for breakfast. I hope all is well with you this fine morning." Mary had dipped

13

down in a curtsey upon her sister's recognition and replied with the usual, "Good morning, Your Majesty." The table had been set for two just like Anne had asked, and the smells of fresh baked pastries and smoked ham filled the room.

Each sister took her place opposite one another. When both were settled, Anne bowed her head, and Mary followed suit. "Gracious and loving Father, we give thanks for thy bounty we are about to receive. We humbly ask that your loving grace fill the walls of His Majesty's court, and that we may receive the mercies of your kindness. Amen." It was no secret that the Boleyn family practiced the Protestant faith, and since the Act of Supremacy, signed in 1534, which declared Henry the *Supreme Head of the Church of England*. Most of the Catholic churches and monasteries had been stripped of their wealth and power, filling the royal coffers that had begun to dwindle under the pope's authority.

"Why, if the king is the head of the church, must we still observe Catholic rituals?" Mary asked in a low whisper.

"Because, dear sister, His Majesty, even though separated from the Catholic Church and not believing everything that it portrays, still wants all services and public prayers observed in the old ways. After all, he remains a Catholic at heart. You and I both know his marriage to the late queen was against God's law according to the Bible, and that the only way to free his soul, and ease his conscience from his father's proclamations, was to break with Rome. All of his father's advisors were determined to carry on with Henry VII's laws and traditions, having my poor husband feeling trapped and constricted under the

14

Church's authority. I merely showed him that kings are appointed by God himself, and answering to any counsel over our Lord and Savior was simply from the workings of mankind."

The Act of Supremacy had taken a couple of years to achieve. In doing so, many people were either imprisoned, persecuted, or put to death. Cardinal Woolsey had been one to fall short of performing his duties to the king, and now he was dead. Anne had never really cared for the cardinal. She could see right through his schemes way before Henry ever could. Along with her father, the Earl of Wiltshire, and her uncle, the Duke of Norfolk, Henry managed to gather evidence against the late cardinal, showing that he was pocketing more of the crown's money than filling the royal coffers. While the loyalty of the cardinal was pursued, Henry had entrusted him with achieving an annulment from Catherine of Aragon, in hopes that in doing so, Woolsey's life might be spared along with a sliver of what dignity he had left. But true to the late cardinal's fashion, all his pleas for redemption came far too late. Woolsey's fate was permanently sealed when he failed to convince the pope and the clergy that Henry's pleas for a divorce were by all accounts, valid and most important. The Catholic Church had dismissed an audience with the Cardinal not once, but twice, in his petitions to plead the king's case. But Anne and the late cardinal never really had a good rapport to start with.

Their awkward and sometimes heated relationship had begun fourteen years ago. Anne had come back to English court with her sister, Mary, at the request of the king.

1522

It was springtime, and the king had found himself in Mary's bed after remarks made by King Francis. Both girls had been Ladies in Waiting to the French king's wife, Queen Claude. While their mother had tried to instill good and moral values into both her daughters in order to keep their piety, the French court was overflowing with adultery and loose morals. Anne took to heart everything her mother had cautioned her about before entering Queen Claude's household, but poor Mary fell into the wrong crowds almost instantly. While in service, the beautiful French queen had made sure that each of her ladies received the best education in a broad range of subjects. Anne was taught how to sing, dance, and play several types of instruments. She was also well informed how to use her femininity in conversations of political views, as well as flirtation, to get what she wanted.

"Never be caught off guard by a man's ability to flatter his way into your heart. Your maidenhead is of the most important gifts God gave for a woman to have. Therefore, she must not give it up quickly." Queen Claude was a very wise woman, probably more so than her philandering husband.

Shortly after Anne and her sister entered into Queen Catherine's household, a tall, handsome and intelligent young man by the name of Henry Percy caught Anne's affections. Young Percy was the heir to the Earl of Northumberland, and while Anne had been away, had been betrothed to Mary Talbot. Anne thought Percy's betrothed rather too submissive, and she seemed to know nothing about how to keep a man's attention through general conversation.

"Honestly, Percy, I cannot put my finger on it, that is to say, what makes Mary Talbot so interesting? She surely has station, and she's pretty in her own way, but she doesn't seem to spark your interest otherwise." Percy would smile, and with his wide, cat-like grin, beguile her with his reply.

"Sweet Anne, it's not that I want to marry her at all. It is my father's doing, and I've been very forthcoming about my feelings concerning this union. I have told him my affections lie elsewhere, but he insists that in time, love will soon follow the exchange of our wedding vows."

Anne would play coy and ask the already known answer to her silent question. "Oh, sweet Percy, for whom do your affections yearn?"

"Anne, you know it is you I desire. I have arranged for us to meet with Cardinal Woolsey tomorrow morning to dissolve my contract with the Lady Talbot and gain the approval for our marriage." While saying this, he had slipped a square-cut ruby ring onto her left hand. Anne looked down at it and then looked at Percy. The ring was beautiful and must have been a family heirloom.

"Oh, my sweetest love, if it were left up to my answer and my answer only, I would have no hesitation in saying yes. So for now, consider my answer to be just that, yes, and once we are granted permission to proceed with our union, we shall begin our new lives."

But the couple's new beginning would never take root. When they entered into Cardinal Woolsey's chambers the next morning, they were not only a party of three. Percy's father, Mary Talbot's father (the Fourth Earl of Shrewsbury), along with Anne's father and uncle, were in attendance, as well. Sir Thomas Moore, the king's lawyer and close friend, also attended the meeting. Cardinal Woolsey sat behind an elaborate wooden desk that had a golden cross, and stacks of parchment paper off to one side. His hands were folded together, showing off his cardinal's ring, resting on a long scroll that had been undone earlier so that the edges did not roll up. The atmosphere was a somber one, and Anne knew what was about to be said. She placed her arm through her love's, and their hands met in unison.

"Henry Percy, you and the Lady Anne Boleyn have been summoned here to mute any indiscretions there may be about your signed betrothal to Mary Talbot. The king has graciously provided you with a very suitable match befitting your station in addition to an inheritance from your father. And though I don't know all there is to know when it comes to young love, I do know that neither the king nor the pope is willing to tolerate such disobedience regarding this matter." Anne could sense the heat rising from her body, and felt a strong urge to let the plump and pompous cardinal hear her fury. But with a quick glance in her father's direction, she thought better against it.

"Cardinal Woolsey, is there no other way for this delicate matter to be resolved? Am I to be an unhappy husband?" Percy asked. He had released Anne's hand by now and was using his own hands in a gesture of pleading.

But to no avail, the two love-struck youths were ultimately outnumbered and out ruled, by not one—but two—higher powers. Before leaving Woolsey's chambers, Anne, who was being ushered out by her father, managed to glance back over her shoulder and lock eyes with the settled clergyman. She glared at him so intently that she hoped he felt her fury deep within his cold, black heart. After a quick hug and a few shed tears, Anne removed the ruby ring from her hand and gave it back to Percy, and just like that, he was gone.

January, 1536

After they had finished eating, Mary helped Anne dress for morning mass. By now, the sounds and smells of vendors and spectators filled the air. Excitement seemed to find its way into the palace, and everyone, including all of Anne's ladies, were giddy with anticipation. She had given leave for a few of them to go and enjoy the day's festivities. Some ladies had husbands that were participating in events, while others had never even seen a jousting tournament before. Anne had requested her red velvet gown, trimmed with white pearls and red rubies, to show her support of the Tudor rose of which she now was a part. "Please don't lace the bodice too tight. I want the people to see not just their queen, but the prince she carries. It will no doubt please His Majesty greatly that our unborn son is growing so quickly." As she said this, a sharp pain, one she had felt when she last miscarried, seared through her stomach. *Stay calm, Anne, it's merely your growing child thriving in anticipation of hearing his father's voice.* She kept this little conversation to herself.

19

She dared not let anyone see her in any discomfort or distress.

Mary placed a strand of rubies and pearls on the crown of Anne's head, and against her dark, raven colored hair, they made her look positively regal, a true queen.

"Ready, sister?" Mary asked, and with a quick look in the mirror, a sincere smile and slight nod, the Queen of England was headed out of her chambers with four of her ladies, including her sister, to join the king for morning prayers.

Chapter Two

"No more to you at this present mine own darling for lack of time but that I would you were in my arms or I in yours for I think it long since I kissed you. By the hand of him which I trust shortly shall be yours." - Henry R.

1526

How did I, Anne Boleyn, catch the eye of the King of England? I am merely an average woman of no great distinction. But here I stand, close enough to smell the ale on his breath. He is a very graceful dancer, and no matter how hard I try, his eyes follow me everywhere I go. "Tell me, fair lady, what your name is, for I must know it." His words sounded hungry and somewhat wanting. It was rather exciting and made her feel like a bird in flight. "Anne Boleyn, Your Majesty, I am the daughter of the Earl of Wiltshire and sister to Mary Boleyn of whom Your Majesty has known before me."

"My Lady Anne, I have to be completely honest, I knew your name already, but I wanted to hear if your voice sounded as sweet as your disposition seems to be." Henry leaned in closer to her, and when he was nearly close enough to kiss her neck, he inhaled deeply and released his consumption of her smell upon her bare neck. "Heaven help me," Anne prayed silently. She had managed to keep her virginity intact for many years, but this man, if he truly pursued her like he insinuated through his body language and words, it was going to be very challenging not to give in like her sister Mary had done. "You must join me for a hunt or a card game soon. I must become more acquainted with such an intoxicating woman. Do you consent to this?" He asked tenderly.

Anne, remembering her education in France, thought for a moment. With a shy and flirtatious demeanor, she conceded to Henry's request. "As My Lord wishes, but I do have one request. Either my father or brother George should be present. I would not want anyone putting rumors around court that I was your mistress. It would certainly ruin any future prospects for a marriage." At first, Henry's face was that of a spoiled child who had been told *no,* but he quickly replaced his dislike for her request with a beautiful and friendly smile. "Anything for you, Lady Anne."

January, 1536

Walking down the long corridors of Greenwich Palace seemed to take forever. Along the way, Anne made sure that she cradled her belly while she nodded to every "Good morning, Your Majesty." It was not so long ago that she had been pregnant with her second child and walking these same halls to mass every morning to ask for a healthy male heir. But unfortunately, that pregnancy was not meant to be, because only weeks after confirmation, she had been violently awakened by pains so great she thought she would surely die. It had all happened so quickly, and within mere moments, her pregnancy had been no more. The shock of it all had left Anne confused and determined that she was still with child. But after the physicians and midwives had examined her and cleaned up all the evidence of any child, Anne had been faced with the heartache that her baby, possibly her son, was no longer.

Henry, while emotionally disappointed, had come to Anne's chambers, after she had been bathed and dressed to receive him, to pass on his condolences for her loss.

"But My Lord, it was a loss for us both, was it not?" She had not been able to hold back the tears that had been waiting, ever so patiently, to fall down her face. "I'm so very sorry, my love. I was so careful, so positive in thought. I don't know why or understand the root of this misfortune." She had covered her eyes and had begun to weep harder. Henry had come to her bedside and sat down. He had placed one finger under her chin and lifted her head until her eyes meet his.

"Sweetheart, I am just as distraught as you are. Am I not a human being first and only king second? We are both still young, and obviously fertile, to try again once you have recovered." He had leaned closer to her and wrapped his long arms around her, pulling her limp body to him to receive his comforting embrace.

Finally, she arrived at the king's chapel, where Henry and other nobility were gathered for prayer. Henry met

Anne at the entryway and held out his arm for her to take hold. Almost in unison, the two walked silently to the front of the tiny chapel, where a priest was standing in wait. "Your Majesties," he greeted them both and nodded for them to kneel down on the velvet cushions that had been placed there for their comfort. The tiny room was packed, but you could hear a pin drop, had someone tossed one to the stone floor.

"In nomine Patris, et Filii, et Spiritus Sancti, Amen." *In the name of the Father and of the Son, and of the Holy Spirit, Amen.* The ceremony had commenced with everyone making the sign of the cross while the priest opened the room for prayer. Most protestants were fully against upholding this Catholic ritual, but Anne wanted to show everyone, especially her husband, that she was a loving and devoted wife and queen. "Heavenly Father, I humbly beseech you to place your protection and grace upon every soul here. Be with our beloved and most gracious king as he competes in today's tournaments. Be also with our devoted and loving queen as she carries the future prince. We thank you for your forgiveness and never-ending love for us, your humble servants. We also thank you for the victories that our king will provide for all of Christendom to remember for all time, Amen.

After making the sign of the cross again and partaking of Communion, everyone began to move about the chapel and disperse to the day's festivities. Henry being the true gentleman or showman, depending how you looked at it, helped Anne to her feet.

"My beautiful queen, I trust you had a peaceful night's sleep? You look well rested, but I still think it best for you and my unborn son to rest today. There is no need for you to worry your pretty little head over my safety when it's my turn to joust." He brought one of her hands to his lips and ever so gently kissed it.

"Whatever you think is best, my love. I shall do as you command and wait to hear news of your victory. I've had my ladies make ready my window seat so I can listen to the cheers as you take to the tilt yard." Anne pulled her hand free from Henry's and reached inside a secret pocket that had been specially sewn in her skirts, pulling out a gold ribbon.

"Here, my love, I have made a beautiful favor for you to tie around your lance." Henry took the shiny piece of ribbon and saw where Anne had stitched her motto: "The most happy," on one side, and her initials, "AB," on the other.

"Sweetheart, this is most kind and thoughtful of you. I shall treasure it always. Even when I am not participating in tournaments, I shall carry it on my person at all times as a reminder of the woman who loves me so." He tucked the token of good luck inside his tunic and wrapped his arms around her, pulling her closer to him. Without warning, he bent down and kissed her deeply. The kiss was so passionate that Anne thought she might have swooned, had he not held her in his embrace. After what seemed like minutes, Henry drew back from her and stood up straight. Both their cheeks were flushed with desire, but the king quickly regained his composure, realizing that everyone was staring at them. "Henry, since when have you ever shied away from showing public affection towards me?" The king looked at her with loving eyes and a boyish grin. "Anne, I cannot be distracted from my thoughts today. I have full intentions of winning this tournament in your honor," he said sincerely.

1526

Henry, or Harry, as those closest to the king called him, was by all accounts a very attractive man. When Anne had first laid eyes on her future husband, it was in Calais when both the English and French courts had come together for a royal summit that would increase the bond of friendship between the two monarchs. It was also known as the Field of the Cloth of Gold, and no expense had been spared by either king to show just how powerful they both were. There were huge feasts, every table filled with smoked meats and pastries. A fountain was even designed and built to have only wine pouring from each spout. Anne was a young girl, but she had managed herself with the demeanor and grace of a mature woman. Her father, Thomas, had managed to persuade King Francis to let both his daughters attend the gathering. He wanted to place his daughters in the path of the English king in hopes that their natural beauty and education would catch his eye.

"Just remember who you truly are, the daughters of a nobleman of the English court. Wear your finest gowns, ones that sparkle and shine. Be gracious, but cautious, because there will be a lot of men there just waiting to fill your pretty heads with sweet words of empty promises. Use the lessons the French queen has instilled in you, and make sure to introduce yourself to His Majesty, King Henry." Both Anne and Mary were left with mixed feelings of excitement and confusion. Why was it so important for two ladies in waiting to place themselves in the English king's attendance? "Mary, why does Father insist that we make ourselves known to the King of England? You have been promised to William Stafford I, too, will soon have male suitors and then a proper match for marriage."

"Silly Anne, my betrothal is still a few years away, and who knows, some other male courtier may pursue his luck for my hand in marriage. I would not mind being a duchess. Besides, father says that we are to return to our home at Hever. It will be nice to be back in our normal surroundings and seeing mother again." Anne watched her sister pull out several gowns from their trunks and spread them across their pallet. *Why does a girl have to try so hard to catch a husband? Do women stay so low in society that they almost have to be whored out to get a decent offer?* She kept these thoughts to herself, because Mary, even after her betrothal had been arranged, had managed to become King Francis's mistress.

At first, Anne had not wanted to believe the idle gossip that had consumed the French court, until she overheard a group of Queen Claude's senior ladies discussing how distasteful it was that the king showed no discretion or respect for his wife by parading that *Boleyn girl* everywhere he went. "Why, he practically fornicates right in public not caring how upset it makes the queen feel."

"Mary, why must you concede to idle gossip that follows your name? Are you truly sleeping with the king? Does that not bother you in the least that Queen Claude had placed her trust in you as a Lady of her household only for you to give in to the king's kind words and trinkets of affection? If father knew you

27

were whoring yourself around court and especially with the king, he would, well, he might be forced to send you to a convent."

"A woman has to make her own way in this world, and I do not intend on becoming a farmer's wife. Besides, I'm quite sure Father knows my indiscretions and says nothing, because through my sinful nature, we have gained status and wealth to place us in the English court." Anne, finding this very distasteful and unethical, decided right then and there that a little harmless flirtation would not hurt or diminish her virtue. But she would not, even if the world was offered to her, stoop as low as her sister had done. There are many ways to achieve a heart's desires, but sleeping one's way through them was not for her.

January, 1536

Before Henry turned to leave, Anne suddenly felt the urge to prolong his departure for just a few moments more.

"My Lord, I had my ladies prepare me a comfortable spot on the window seat so that I can listen to all the cheers the people will no doubt express for their beloved king. If I listen hard enough, maybe I will be able to hear when they announce you. So know that your son and I will be cheering you on."

Anne gave her husband a sincere smile and dipped down into a slight courtesy. Being with child, she was not expected to show this sign of respect because of the risk of falling or losing one's balance, but she felt compelled to do it anyway. Henry was back at her side in seconds, lifting her back to a standing position. "Anne, have you lost your senses? You know that I dislike anything that could potentially harm our unborn son. Now please, allow your ladies to escort you back to your chambers, get comfortable, rest if you must, and wait for my return this evening with victory in my hands." He gave her another kiss on her forehead and nodded to Mary and Nan to take his queen to her rooms. "'Til later, my love," he said with a bow. "'Til later," Anne replied with a smile.

The walk back to her chambers seemed much shorter this time, because most of the court had already left for the tilt yard. The only people around were servants, sweeping and dusting tapestries and rugs from the many rooms at Greenwich Palace. Though the king had many palaces in his possession, Greenwich was one of his favorites. That's why he had the tilt yard and arena built here. Most of the court followed them with each new season to another palace, in which they would stay for as long as Henry saw fit. Whether it was because he wanted to leave the hustle and bustle of courtly life at Hampton court to spend most of his time hunting wild game around Ludlow Castle, or merely to relax at Anne's childhood home at Hever, it would take at least two to three days of planning and packing in order for the royal court to move from one place to the next.

Henry had a reason for everything, it seemed. While he greatly enjoyed hosting lavish celebrations which had plenty of wine and ale for almost the whole of England, he was a very superstitious monarch, as well. Case in point, the devastating outbreak of the sweating sickness in June of 1528. Anne remembered this period

29

in time very well. She had been removed from Queen Catherine's services, because Henry had hoped to persuade her to be his one true mistress. He had given Anne her own private rooms at court and visited her regularly—with her father or brother present, of course.

The court had been in the full swing of daily activities when one of Anne's ladies had started complaining of a headache. She was promptly dismissed to go lie down in hopes that some much-needed rest would cure her throbbing head. Within a few hours, the young girl had died. When Henry had received word from Anne that one of her ladies had died under curious conditions, he had summoned a physician to make inquiries to what might have happened to the poor girl. When word had come back that several others had complained of the same symptoms and that they too had shortly died, Henry had quickly made plans to leave court.

He had sent word to Anne that the sweating sickness had made its way through the whole of Europe, and that he wanted her to return home to Hever for her safety. He promised that he would write often to check on her and to keep her abreast of any new developments. Henry had also commanded that Catherine and the Princess Mary be packed and made ready to leave for the country for their safety, as well. Before leaving, Anne had sent a letter to Henry. She had heard that Catherine and Mary would be leaving with the king and she did not want to leave court without letting Henry know how much she loved him.

My dearest and most gracious Majesty,

I hope that this letter finds you well and in good spirits. I am leaving as you commanded, for my father's home in hopes to escape this horrible sickness that has befallen your kingdom. Please know that you will be in every prayer I say and every thought that crosses my mind. Even while we are separated, for however long, know that my love will not be diminished or dismayed. I already miss your embrace and the sound of your sweet voice but I know that you are with me in my own heart, never to leave it. Know that I shall be ever so wanting to be with you and will cling to every letter you send to me. Stay well my love and know my heart is yours.

With all the love that I possess,

Anne Boleyn

And after the page boy left with her letter in hand, Anne had quickly gathered her belongings and with her father, settled into a carriage that had been prepared for them to begin their journey to Hever Castle.

It was not long after Anne and her father had settled down in the safe confines of their home that Anne had begun to feel unwell. She had been stirred from her sleep by a pounding headache and shortly after, her whole body had been drenched in sweat. The sickness had come so quickly that she had no time to write her beloved a letter letting him know of her illness. Her brother George had sent word to the king that both his sister and father had contracted the sweat and that they were being cared for.

Your Majesty, I write this letter with the gravest news. My sister Anne along with my father has both become very ill. My mother and I are caring for them and pray consistently for their recovery. My poor sister Mary has lost her husband, William

Carey, just this morning and while Mary shows no signs of the illness, she too has decided to stay in her home for fear that she might further contaminate our household. I will write as often as I can to keep you informed of any changes in my sister's condition. We pray that your Majesty and Queen Catherine are well and we hope that this sickness will soon disperse from your lands. Always your humble servant,

George Boleyn

Henry, fearing that his beloved might die, insisted that his personal physician go to Hever Castle and tend to the Lady Anne and her father. "Make sure My Lady recovers with haste. Treat her as if she were my own wife." Within a few days, Anne's fever had broken, and she began feeling much better. Her father, who had also been ill, had made a full recovery a couple days before his daughter. Anne had felt as weak as a newborn, but she had insisted on sending word to His Majesty that she had pulled through, and that she yearned ever so much to see his face.

Chapter Three

January, 1536

"Your Grace, we have prepared you a very comfortable pallet for you to comfortably listen to the day's festivities. We even made sure that plenty of food and drink be brought, some from vendors on the grounds so you can enjoy what others are getting, too." Her cousin, Madge, sounded excited and very pleased with herself with all the work she had done while Anne had been away at prayer.

"Cousin Madge, how wonderful everything looks! You are too kind, and very much appreciated. I can always trust in you for making me smile." At that moment, Anne felt that stabbing pain run through her belly again. This time, it felt a little stronger than the last. She let out a small moan as she rubbed her swollen belly in hopes that her caress would soothe the babe within her womb.

"Anne, are you alright?" Mary asked. "Do I need to summon the midwife or the physician?" Anne quickly dismissed her sister's inquiries and reassured all her ladies that she was fine. "The little prince must be telling me that I have done too much already. Mary, could you please help me change into my loose-fitting gown? I think I would feel better if I was not confined by these laces." She began pulling at the ribbon that was holding the red velvet sleeves in place. With each tug, the heavy gown started to come apart. She loved wearing elaborate gowns and jewels for her beloved, but when there was another person to carry underneath it all, being laced up and tucked in was not at all pleasant. If she could, she would prefer to wear her cotton chemise and dressing gown everyday if it were befitting. Since it was not, Anne could only suffer in silence and pray for a quick appearance until she was back in her rooms and behind closed doors.

As her sister unlaced her skirts, Anne secretly checked her lace chemise for any signs of blood. "Oh, thank God, there is no evidence of blood. Anne, could you be still? I have but one more lace to untie before you are free from this frock." Mary said, almost breathless. "You need to lie down, sister, maybe rest for a while. This morning has no doubt taken its toll on you and the child. I will come wake you when I hear His Majesty's name being called, or if a messenger comes with word of his victories." Mary gathered each piece of the gown in her arms, laying them neatly in a chair. Since the garment had not been worn for a long period of time, it would be hung back in the queen's closet until it was needed again.

"Thank you, dear sister, but I will take my rest by the window seat. Our cousin has outdone herself to make me a most comfortable spot in which I can enjoy hearing the day's events or closing my eyes for a quick nap. Either way, I'll feel like I'm a part of the festivities." Nan pulled out a rose gold colored gown that was made of satin. It was a very beautiful gown and even more comfortable. She had worn it when she was pregnant with Elizabeth. "Thank you, Nan. I feel much better." Anne slipped her feet into her soft gold slippers and proceeded to the front parlor. She looked around at her ladies, who had all settled into their needle work and noticed that one of her ladies was not there.

"Where is the Lady Jane Seymour? Was she not instructed to be in my service today? I do not remember granting her the day off." As she looked around the room, all she saw were solemn faces amongst her ladies. They were trying very hard to deflect their queen's inquiries, but to no avail. Anne asked again, but this time, she singled out a lady by name. One she knew could not tell a lie, even if she was commanded to.

"Cousin Madge, why is it that no one seems to know where the Lady Jane has disappeared to? Surely you, of all my ladies, would not harbor any secrets from not only your cousin but queen?" Madge's face had turned pale after the first question was asked, but now became crimson with embarrassment at being singled out. And true to form, she could not lie about where the missing lady was. It must have been a monstrous ordeal to keep this information a secret, because all the other ladies kept their eyes on their work at hand and dared not look directly at Anne.

"Your Grace, early this morning before you were awake, a messenger arrived with a letter from his Majesty requesting that Lady Jane accompany you to mass but stay behind afterwards for his pleasure. While you and His Majesty were deep in prayer, Sir Thomas

35

Cromwell escorted Lady Jane to His Majesty's chambers and had another of your ladies take her place. We were made to promise to act as if nothing was amiss under pain of punishment. So in order not to upset you, Your Grace, we have tried not to bring attention to her absence."

Anne's cousin could not look her in the eye, so she knew that Madge was telling her the honest truth.

"Nan, fetch me my coverlet. I must go to His Majesty's chambers at once. The jousting has just begun, and I know that Henry usually does not joust until the tournament is well under way." She could feel the heat of anger rise from far within her soul. *I'll catch him in the act and see to it that the Lady Jane Seymour is sent back to her father's house, if it's the last thing I do today.*

As she swung open the door to her rooms, she could feel an achy twinge of pain pierce her heart. Why does he do this especially when he knows how delicate my condition is? Is he so confident that I will not bear him a son? Regardless of whether I am carrying a prince or another princess, I do not deserve to be treated in such a manner. I will not bow down as my predecessor had done before me. She remembered a time when Henry was in hot pursuit for her affections.

As she made her way down the corridors that led to Henry's chambers, she recalled a love letter he had written her while she was spending time at Hever to escape all the dirty looks and whispers that were circulating around Whitehall about her supposed affair with Henry.

Mine own sweetheart, these shall to be to advertise you of the great loneliness that I find here since your departing... Wishing myself (specially an evening) in my sweetheart's arms, whose pretty dukkys I trust shortly to kiss. Written by the hand of him that was, is, and shall be yours by his will. - H.R.

How is it that a man's affections can waver so much and so often? Was her love, and her love alone, not enough to pacify him? She soon found her way to Henry's chambers. Two armed guards stood at the ready, and both looked very much caught off guard to see her there. "Step aside. I need to have an audience with my husband before he heads to the tournaments." Her tone must have frightened them both, for there was no hesitation when both men stepped aside to let her pass. Just as she had thought, there in front of God and herself, sat the king with the frail, pale-faced Jane Seymour sitting on his lap letting Henry steal kisses from her swollen pink lips.

"How dare you find yourself alone in my husband's arms! That place is reserved only for the Queen of England, and I do not recall being stripped of that title. Get up, you little back stabbing wench. I'll have you flogged and sent home disgraced, to your father's home, if I need to." Just then, a sharp, searing pain surged through Anne's belly and left her gasping for air. Seeing this, Henry instructed Jane to leave promptly. He called out for the physician. He made his way to Anne's side and wrapped his arms around her so if she fainted, she would not hit the floor.

"Anne, my darling wife, calm yourself, if not for your sake, do so for our unborn son." Henry tightened his grip on her a little more as Anne slowly slumped to the floor in protest. "Oh Henry, how could you? I'm your wife, the love you had pined for over seven years, and I patiently waited through them all with the hope in this world that you would love me with the same passion as I do for you. My heart has beats only for you. Why can't yours do the same, Henry? Tell me why!" She was sobbing now, and the pain was so great that she felt faint. Henry must have realized her distress. He picked her up in his arms and carried her with haste back to her chambers.

After the physician had examined her, he came from behind the drawn curtains of her bedchamber to reassure the king. As of now, Anne was still with child, but the day's events had been too much for Her Majesty.

"I have instructed her ladies to make her rest in the bed for a while. We placed some pillows under her swollen feet to relieve the pressure. Her heart is racing, but there is no sign of fever or distress to the child. Your Majesty may go in, but say nothing to upset her. Then after you've enjoyed your tournament, you may return to see your wife."

Henry thanked the physician for his hastiness in attending the queen. He slowly pulled back the curtain to enter where Anne lay sleeping. He went and knelt down beside her and placed his hand upon her swollen belly. "Oh, my dearest, please don't be too harsh with me. I never meant to upset you or endanger my unborn son. Please forgive me; I am but a foolish man, a selfish man. I am the one who needs to be flogged and punished. Will you concede to forgive my indiscretions?"

"Your groveling does nothing but lessen your apology, My Lord." Anne replied, opening her eyes to look at him. "Thank you for your kindness in making sure I did not hit the floor, for I think that it would have furthered my pain. Besides, it was merely a kiss, was it not? Surely, I, your queen, can overlook a young girl's fantasy of being kissed by the king, can I not? Win this tournament in our unborn son's name, and all shall be forgiven. But only if you save your victory kisses for my lips only." Anne gave Henry a little half smile.

She watched as his face, filled with worry, turned into the handsome young king smiling, because he had managed to escape a mousetrap. "Now, be gone, My Lord, leave us be. While you are showing our people just how strong and noble you are, I must rest and grow your son inside my aching womb." Henry kissed her hand. After he stood up, ever the gentleman, bowed to his queen and bade her farewell.

The darkness once again surrounded her, but the air felt much heavier than it had before. Once again, she could hear muffled sounds coming from somewhere. As hard as she tried, she could not see from whom or where it was coming. Never being one to hold her patience for too long, Anne felt herself being moved towards something. And as she approached, she could hear the sounds more clearly now.

"Who is there? Speak up; this is your queen, and I demand to know who is in my rooms." But no one answered. The sound grew louder still, so she cleared her throat, hoping that in doing so, the person—or persons—would either acknowledge her or leave her in peace. But her effort was to no avail, and she found

39

herself at the same door she had encountered in her dream the night before.

"Your Majesty, I can assure you that I will leave no page left unturned. I will work most diligently on this matter and have your evidence before two days' time." It was Lord Cromwell's voice. She'd recognize it even in the darkest of nights. "Good, then I can move forward with my engagement and upcoming marriage. Once you've made enquiries about these disturbing accusations against Queen Anne, that is." Henry chuckled a most hair-raising laugh, and Anne could feel all the blood drain from her body. *Accusations? Enquiries? What were they talking about? And why did Henry say against me, Anne Boleyn?* The two men seemed to know someone was listening in on their conversation, and the discussion ended there.

"Wake up Anne, wake up." But apparently, her dream was not yet finished with her. *After what seemed like an eternity, she found herself back at Hever Castle. It looked like springtime, because the wildflowers were in full bloom. She was standing in her bedroom, staring at herself in front of her mirror. She was wearing a deep green silk and damask gown that was adorned with pearls. Her long black hair was braided and placed inside a green laced net that lay beneath the deeper green veil of her French hood.*

"Anne, my sweetheart, it is I, your Henry. I have come to call on you." She twirled around to see Henry standing at her doorway, staring at her with such a hunger that she was sure he was envisioning her naked. Her heart began to quicken with the thought of giving in to his demands and letting both of them enjoy the fruits of their desires, but she quickly dismissed the notion and curtsied in acknowledgement. "My Lord, you have taken me by surprise. I knew you were coming, but standing in

my room nearly out of breath—because you took the steps two at a time, I'm guessing, simply to see if you could catch a glimpse of me not fully clothed. Shame on you." Anne giggled, knowing that teasing him in this way drove his desire for her deeper each day. Henry rushed over and lifted her up into his arms, pulling her mouth onto his. Their kiss became ever more intense with each second. I remember this day. Oh, how devoted and besotted he was for my affections. Even though this was a dream of days gone past, she could still feel the passion.

"Oh, my love, please let me have one small token of your love before our ride, or I shall think you don't truly love me." Henry pleaded with her like a child would over a pastry. Before she could reply, Henry had placed her on her bed and began kissing her neck. He could be so passionate when he wanted something. The bodice to her gown had been laced a little tighter today in order for her breasts to be pushed up. Not so much that people would call her a harlot, but in the French fashion, which she admired so much. "Leave just enough presented to catch a man's attention but not so much that he doesn't have to guess what lies beneath your gown." Queen Claude had informed them. Within seconds, Henry's hungry lips found the peaked mounds of her bodice and ran his hands over her skin. Anne let out a small moan and soon Henry's lips found their way to the bareness of her neck and bosom.

"Henry my love, you must not spoil anything. We are not yet married, and if I were to let you continue, I'm most certain I could not refuse you any longer." She was panting with desire.

"My annulment will be granted soon. I promise I will not take your maidenhead until our wedding night, but I must feel something sacred to quench my longing for you." His gaze was so intense that she could think of only one thing to do. She bucked her body against his and managed to have him flat on his back. "Here is something to cool your desires for now." Her

hands slid down his tunic and rested on his cod piece. His erection let her know the full extent of his passion. While kissing him ever so deeply, she untied his doublet and reached inside to touch his manhood. Henry groaned in pleasure, and it was not long before his passions were released. Anne made sure that she had her mouth over his to muffle any sounds he made. She did not want anyone to hear them

After Henry had cleaned himself and retied his doublet and cod piece, he kissed Anne feverishly. "My own darling, let me return the favor," he said hungrily, but Anne quickly quieted him by saying, "Later My Lord, later."

Just when she liked her dream and where it was heading, a sharp pain ravaged her body. She sat straight up in her bed. She must have cried out, because her ladies were all in her bedchamber. "Your Majesty, are you all right? Should we send for the physician?"

As she became more aware of her surroundings, she promptly felt under the covers for any trace of blood. *Oh, thank God! No blood, only sweat from my dreams.* "No, I'm alright. Just a bad dream. Is there any word from My Lord? How goes the tournament?" Her sister, Mary, came to her bedside. "No word yet on how things are going. We heard His Majesty's name announced a few times, and the crowd roared with excitement. The clock just struck one, and we still have your window seat ready—if you feel up to sitting for a while. You could probably use something to eat and drink, as well."

My word, one o'clock already? I must have been truly exhausted. "Yes, I will be most excited to join you all in the front parlor for refreshments." She reached for her coverlet and slipped it on along with her slippers from earlier. Her body seemed to protest her movements, but she would do nothing else today that could upset the child she still carried. "Come now, little prince, let us feast on some meats and bread while we listen closely for your father's name to be announced." Anne placed her hand on her belly and smiled. "I'll keep you safe my sweet one. You just continue to thrive, and I'll try to behave. Is that a good deal between the two of us?" She felt a light quickening, reassuring her that the unborn prince was in approval.

STEPHANIE BASCO SULLIVAN

Chapter Four

A nne could feel the fresh afternoon air wash over her as soon as she pulled back the curtain separating her bedchamber from the parlor. Even though it was late in January, the sunlight seemed to warm the cold confines of the Palace to a very tolerable temperature. A scent of smoked meats hit her senses, and her stomach cried out in protest. "My word, is that smell from in here or from the vendors?" She asked hungrily. "We wanted to bring you a surprise, My Lady. So we sent Mary down to buy us some smoked turkey legs and quail eggs for our lunch today." All her ladies were giddy with excitement and very proud of what they had managed to surprise their queen with. "Ladies, you have outdone yourselves. This is one of the sweetest things ever done for me. I'll be sure to commend your services to your king this evening. He will be most pleased, as I am now."

Anne insisted on fixing each lady her own plate as a sign of her gratitude, and with a little hesitation they finally gave in to the queen's generosity. When all the ladies had plates and cups of wine, Anne finished loading her own plate with samples of everything. She did not feel up to drinking wine or ale but wanted a glass of cool water. The wine at breakfast had given her some discomfort, and she wasn't about to cause further of the same. The food tasted so good—so good, in fact, that soon her plate was nearly cleaned. "Heaven help me, that was most delicious. I could not hold another bite even if I wanted to." All her ladies agreed. While the empty plates and napkins were being cleared and taken away by one of the kitchen maids, a loud roar came from the tilt yard. Anne leaned against the window sill to hear who everyone was cheering for. Then when the trumpets sounded, she knew it was Henry who was entering the joust. Her heart leapt with excitement and a little hesitation. Jousting was a very dangerous sport, but it had also been a longstanding tradition among royalty and noblemen for centuries. While in France, she had attended one and found it rather unpleasing when one of the knights was knocked completely off his horse. A sliver of wood had penetrated his chain mail, piercing his left arm. There had been much blood, and most of the women had fainted upon seeing the injured, or worse—the unfortunate souls that died from their injuries.

Jousting had become outlawed in France shortly after, because it was deemed too barbaric. As she looked out the window, Anne watched several people strolling by. She saw a mother holding a little girl around the age of four or five months, and she instantly felt the need to see her Elizabeth.

Anne had not seen her daughter in a fortnight, due to her condition. It was suggested that bed rest for the first couple of weeks was best since Anne had become pregnant so soon after her miscarriage. Not getting to see her own daughter was almost too much to bear. Then her thoughts fell upon another young lady whose mother was being laid to rest this very day.

Catherine of Aragon had been ordered to leave Whitehall Palace in the winter of 1533. The continued arguments, over whether her first marriage to Henry's older brother, Arthur, was ever consummated during their three-month marriage, seemed to be the topic of gossip at court. It also proved to be the biggest obstacle in Henry's desire in getting the pope's consent for his annulment. And even though it was causing a lot of strain on Henry and Anne, she had to give Catherine the benefit of the doubt. The forty-eight-year-old queen had changed profoundly throughout the past few years but had managed to still have all of England's hearts.

Anne had seen and served the former queen in her younger years and thought her quite pretty. But it soon became clear that the queen had no regard towards Anne when Henry forbade the marriage between her newest lady in waiting to Henry Percy, because he had wanted her for himself. At first, Anne had tried to remain mute and unmoved by the queen's temperament towards her. But as Henry's affections grew, so too, did Catherine's anger. One night as Anne was helping the queen ready for bed, she ordered all the other ladies out all except Anne.

"Lady Anne, do not think me so blind as to not see how my husband, the king, spoils you with gifts and tokens of his affections. I come from a long line of strong, independent women who have ruled Spain in spite of their husband's flaws. Do not think for one second that the king's affections have altered so much that he has forgotten me. And never think that you can ever take my place as his wife and queen, because that, my child, has been taken by me." Anne remained silent, but something inside her felt the need to defend herself against Catherine's harsh words.

"With all respect, Your Majesty, I am not asking for His Majesty's affections, nor do I encourage him. I merely dance when he asks me to, or accompany him on a hunt if my father commands it. Who am I to say no to the King of England?"

"I did not permit you to speak. How dare you accuse me of calling you out when it is you who have called me out and made me the talk of the court." Catherine was no longer sitting, but standing, with both hands on her hips with a stare that made Anne's blood run cold. "Do as you must, Lady Anne. Play to his affections, let him take you to his bed if he must, but don't think that he will divorce me to have a common whore as his wife."

"A whore I am not, Your Majesty. I still have my maidenhead and the king knows I am not my sister, Mary. I will do as you bid me, but as for His Majesty, I will be by his side if he asks me."

Anne curtsied and turned to leave before things really got out of hand, but Catherine had other plans in mind. "I did not give you permission to leave. We are not finished here. I have given the king a long and happy marriage and friendship for almost twenty-four years. I have borne his children. I have shared in everything that his heart desired, but I will not let anyone take my place. Only God can remove me from Henry's side."

"You gave him one living child, Your Grace. A daughter, I believe, and I have heard it said that you bleed no more. You may have carried six of His Majesty's heirs but only one remains, a daughter, and I do believe a son is required to keep the Tudor line going."

"How dare you!" Catherine yelled and without warning, the queen had made it over to where Anne was standing. She swiftly slapped Anne across her face.

The force behind her strike let Anne know she had gone too far. And for the sake of her position and for the love she now had for the king, she apologized. "I am most sorry, my queen. I meant no insult towards you or your departed children. If my Lady needs nothing more I shall retire for the night." She waited silently as Catherine looked her up and down one last time before dismissing her.

January, 1536

"Catherine of Aragon was laid to rest today, was she not?" she asked in hesitation. She had known that the late queen's funeral would be held this week but she wanted to make sure of the day. "Yes, Your Grace, she was interred this morning, I believe, at Peterborough Cathedral." Mary replied. Anne could not help but feel some piece of sadness; after all, it was not Catherine's choice to make her a lady in her household but that of the king's. After this morning's events, she completely understood how Catherine had felt every time Henry decided to take on another mistress. "Was the Lady Mary allowed to attend?" "No, my Lady, since neither of them took the Oath of Succession, they were denied any visitation when the late queen was banished from court." Nan's voice trailed off for fear that she may have upset Anne with her words. But Anne did not seem to pay much attention. All she could think about was the terrible nightmare that she had lived through this morning. She had come to realize it was she, herself, that was laid in the wooden box, and her ladies were the only attendants.

She remembered that cold day in December, when Henry had become so beside himself with frustration over his divorce.

June, 1529

He had offered Catherine an early retirement either to one of his estates, with a pension and household befitting her station (which was now Dowager Princess of Wales), or relinquish all ties to the royal title and retire to a nunnery of her choice. Of course, Catherine refused both offers and even went as far as making a fool out of herself in court by falling to her knees and begging Henry to have mercy on her for being a true and loyal wife.

"I cannot believe she would debase herself to such humiliation; a queen, crawling around on her hands and knees in front of the court, asking for my reconciliation."

Anne could tell Henry had been beside himself with uncertainty. "My love, she only does these things to anger you. She is no fool; you know that. She's going to stand firm as long as God allows her to breathe. Let us go away for a few weeks; perhaps a hunt, or to visit other estates. Maybe a change in scenery will renew your spirits." Anne always managed to know exactly what to say, and when it needed to be said. So she had decided that it was past time that Henry knew the real reasons as to why he was not getting his divorce.

"I would like to share with you a book that my chaplain, Archbishop Cranmer, showed to me. I think that it can help shed some light on how to get what you want, when you want it." Anne had gone to her bookcase and removed a simple covered book with the title, *The Obedience of the Christian Man,* by William Tyndale. "I think you will find that the men in your council have not your interest or soul's peace in mind, but that of the pope's and Catherine's instead. Tyndale enforces that God appoints all kings, not the pope or mankind, and that the king, himself, needs only to answer to God himself. The Catholic Church has distorted your mind for so many years, and now, when you have considered your eternal soul's place in Heaven through scripture, no less, they find you in the wrong. You should answer to no one but yourself and to God. You deserve happiness here and in the future." She had handed the book to Henry, who had looked it over with eagerness.

"Anne, sweet Anne, can I not have you now? If this is the answer to our prayers, and we have promised ourselves in marriage, can we not share one another?" He had asked with such a passion that it was torture for her to refuse his advancements. "Not yet, my darling, but soon, and I will give you a son shortly after our wedding vows. This I promise."

For a second, Henry had looked as though he might get angry with her, but instead of arguing, he'd asked her to read aloud to him the most important phrases of this mysterious book. Anne had agreed, but he did have one request and had told her she could not refuse him. "While you read to me how we are to achieve or desires, I want to show you my gratitude for calming my anger over my 'Great matter.'" Without warning, Henry had run his hands up under her skirts until he found her thighs. "Start reading" he had commanded. As she had begun reading, she could feel Henry's fingers, hungrily searching for her womanhood. It had been excruciating to read with greedy fingers perusing her very essence. She let out a slight moan when she had realized that it was no longer Henry's fingers that flickered about, but his mouth. "My Lord, I cannot read while you are doing what you are doing."

"Then maybe you should stop until I have finished with my pursuit." Anne could not resist him any longer. She had let Henry explore her entirely until her whole body had frozen with pleasure. A red-faced Henry had uncovered his face from her skirts and begun kissing her neck. "Oh, my sweet Anne, I knew that you would taste just as sweet as your disposition." Anne had reeled in the aftermath of his gratitude.

While she remained on the bed, Henry had gently risen, taking the book out of her hands. "I think I shall do a little light reading before I go to bed tonight. And I do believe that a hunting trip is in order before the Christmas holidays. Oh, and when we return, with the help of this book, no other queen will reside here except you, my darling." And after blowing her a kiss, he had quietly left her rooms, leaving her satisfied and eager for sleep.

Chapter Five

After Henry had read the contents of the book that Anne had given him, he had been even more curious as to what this priest had to say about his "Great Matter." So the king arranged an afternoon tea where he, Anne, and the Archbishop Cranmer could take all the time needed in discussing the way things should be handled. Queen Catherine had already proven to be armed with the backing of Rome and the pope. Therefore, she had no intensions of surrendering easily. During the court proceedings, Queen Catherine had managed to retrieve a valuable and damning piece of evidence that kept the clergy rather hushed on the subject laid before them. "Archbishop Cranmer, Lady Anne tells me that you have a different way of handling my 'great matter' that would place me as a true king. While Queen Catherine has the backing of the pope and her nephew, Charles, she also has in her possession a copy of the papal dispensation issued by Julius II that granted her marriage to Henry whether her first marriage had been consummated or not. What are your words of advice?"

"Well, Your Majesty, you have seen the power of paper testimony but have been lacking in physical evidence proving the validity of the queen's first marriage. I have a couple of men who were in your late brother's service when he and Catherine were married and escorted to their chambers. They have both sworn an oath to be completely honest and forthcoming with everything you brother did or said the morning after his marriage vows. They have agreed to testify on your Majesty's behalf, and much to your favor, that soon, no one can deny that your union was an unholy one, not just according to God's holy word, but through the mouths of those closest to your late brother." Henry had seemed extremely pleased with what Cranmer had to say. He could hardly wait until the court had regained its senses and let Henry have the floor for once. "Your words have moved me into a place of hope and happiness," Henry had said as he reached for Anne's hand; "Soon my darling, so very soon."

January, 1536

Another roar erupted from the tilt yard, seeming to smother the sky, and Anne strained to hear what was happening. But something was not quite right with this new outpouring of excitement. "I wonder what has happened. The people have gone quiet and cheer no more. Madge, would you please go to the yard and make inquiries as to what has caused such a change in celebration?" Her cousin made ready in a matter of seconds and left as quickly as she could manage. "I hope no one is hurt," Anne said with concern.

The rooms had now begun to dim with the setting sun. Anne asked for the candles to be lit and logs added to her fire for the warmth she would no doubt need later that evening. How long had Madge been gone? How long does it take to cross the front gardens that lead straight into the tilt yard? I do believe that I could have already been back with word of what has possibly happened. She could not help but notice that the royal guard had been summoned for the protection of the king, and this worried Anne. But just as she had been taught in France, never show weakness in the face of the unknown. A Lady should always pray for the best but prepare for the worst with dignity and decorum. Just as Anne was about to send another one of her ladies, the door to her chambers was practically knocked down by her clearly distressed cousin.

Madge was trying her best to catch her breath and remain calm in delivering the tidings no wife should ever have to hear. "Lady Madge, what has happened? And do not sugar coat it for my sake. What has happened?" Anne found herself gripping Madge by both her arms and practically shaking the news that would change the future of mankind.

The words seemed to flow from Madge's mouth very slowly. "His Majesty has fallen from his horse and has been crushed."

"What do you mean by saying His Majesty has been crushed? Is he all right? Where is he?" Anne asked with haste.

"Speak, Madge, where is the king?" She was standing up now and had placed her hands on her lady's shoulders. Anne knew that shock could render anyone speechless, but she needed to know exactly what had happened. "Listen to me, cousin; tell me where His Majesty is." Madge started to answer but was silenced by Anne's father and brother George being announced at her door. Both men were dripping with sweat, yet their complexions were as pale as the kiss of death. "Father, tell me what has happened! Is my husband, the king, all right? Will he survive? I must go to him right away." But before she could enter her bedchamber to change her gown, her father followed her to the trunk that had Anne's maternity gowns in it.

"My daughter, please sit first and listen to what I must tell you. His Majesty had entered the jousting contest and when the horses were released and took charge, Sir Henry Norris had the upper hand and knocked the king backwards on his horse. The force in which he was hit was very great indeed, because His Majesty jerked the horse's reigns hard and caused the animal to rare up and fall backwards, landing on the king. The horse quickly got up, and while it looked as though the wind had been knocked out of His Grace, he made no movement. Your brother and I, along with Charles Brandon ran, to be with the king, but when we removed his helmet, he did not open his eyes. We were instructed by the physician to carefully carry the king inside a nearby tent for better evaluation of his injuries. After a few moments, we were told that there was a high possibility that there was head damage along with internal injuries as well. His Majesty has been unconscious for almost an hour now, and his condition does not show signs of improvement." Her father had sat down beside her on the trunk. His hat was in his hands, and he looked like the entire world had been ransacked.

"I must go to him, Father. He needs me. I know he does," she pleaded.

"Anne, I am afraid that at this critical time, and in your condition, it is best to wait just a little bit longer before we rush you to his side. It was highly discussed whether we should even tell you until we knew more, but I insisted that you could at least go to the chapel and pray for your husband."

"But Father, what if he needs me and I am not there? What if something happens and I miss my chance—" She stopped her words short, because it was treason to talk about the king's life, especially if it were a life and death matter. "I shall go to mass, but please send word every half hour on his condition. And if he is moved from the tent to his rooms, do not think to withhold that information from me. I may be your daughter, but I am your queen first. Anne's father nodded in approval and bowed before leaving her chambers.

The sunlight that illuminated her rooms earlier that morning was now completely gone. Anne quickly helped her sister dress her in a somber grey damask gown and placed a black lace veil over her hair. "Quickly, Mary, we must make haste. I want you to attend me to the chapel, but then I want to be alone with my thoughts and prayers. If other courtiers want to pray for their king, they will have to do so in one of the other chapels." Her sister nodded in compliance with Anne's request. After the two sisters were ready to leave, Anne stopped and grabbed her book of hours. Henry had given her this beautiful book of devotion during their courtship. Each page was elaborately decorated with bright colors and gold trim. It truly was one of her most treasured gifts. She had made sure to read it every day and insisted that her household read it whenever they were short on other duties.

"Please begin your prayers for His Majesty's quick recovery. And do not think to have bad or treasonous thoughts, because they are punishable by death. Keep your decorum and respect for your king, myself, and our future prince in this most crucial of times," Anne commanded of her household before she and Mary began their long walk to the king's chapel.

The corridors were packed with courtiers and ambassadors all waiting to hear news of Henry's health. "See how they seize the chance to spread idle gossip even before any acknowledgement of the king's condition has been confirmed?" Anne pointed out to her sister. She remembered that this same group of scavengers, not so long ago, were eagerly waiting to hear what Rome's decision was regarding the king's "Great Matter," and how, in order to keep her name from being smeared any further than it had already been, Henry had sent Anne home to Hever once more until the verdict had been passed.

1529

As Queen Catherine was being summoned to court by the Archbishop, Anne had kissed her beloved Henry goodbye and made herself ready to depart for her father's home. Since Catherine had become quite resilient in resisting Henry's pleas for a quiet and personal dismissal, she had made life for Anne and the king quite unpleasant. Catherine, by all accounts, had refused to show her face in court after her groveling display, and this had not pleased Henry at all.

"Why must she test me so? I have shown her the verse in her precious Bible where it clearly states the reasons I must seek out this annulment." Henry was referring to a passage in the Old Testament of Leviticus Chapter 20; verse 21: "If a man shall take his brother's wife, it is an impurity; he hath uncovered his brother's nakedness; they shall be childless."

"My love, she is but a woman who is strong in her faith but cannot obey her husband as God has commanded. If you were my husband, which I hope surely to be, I, too, would move Heaven and Earth to protect my vanity." Henry had heard the courtiers becoming more impatient with neither monarch present. "I fear I must go, my love. Please send my regards to your father and trust that shortly I shall come for you." He kissed Anne so deeply that her lips had throbbed. He gave her a softer kiss on the hand, and away he went with his Privy Council close behind him. As usual, Anne had wanted to let everyone know that just because she was leaving court for only a little while, she was still held in the highest regard with the king. So she had decided to make her exit a grand affair and one that would be talked about for many years to come. Anne had requested a velvet and damask gown to be made out of the deepest purple. "Leave out no attention to detail, and spare no expense. I expect to have exactly what I want," she had told the dress maker. Purple was a sign of royalty and not permitted to be worn by anyone but His Majesty or the queen. But Anne knew that Catherine's days at court were numbered. She felt it was only fair for her to show everyone just how sure she was of the king's love for her, and she intended to do so by adorning herself as a future queen.

When the coachman came to her rooms at Whitehall, Anne stepped out with all the splendor and dignity of a true queen. Gasps and whispers filled the air, growing louder with each step she took. As she approached the awaiting carriage, she encountered some of Queen Catherine's ladies strolling through the courtyard. One of them sneered, "How dare you wear the color of royal nobility? You should be quite ashamed of yourself prancing about as if you, a common whore, could ever be as splendid as Her Majesty Queen Catherine."

The young lady looked very proud of herself and felt as if she had done a great service to her queen. But Anne, never one to back down when confronted, retaliated with a vengeance while keeping her composure. "Oh, I don't know if it is only I, or if others feel as the king and I, but I could not care less if all Spaniards were lying at the bottom of the sea. For I think the tide is coming in and it is a long way to swim back home, is it not?" She nodded to the young and baffled woman, who had the look of sheer terror on her face.

"Yes, I know, run along, little mouse, and tell your mistress what the great whore has said. But keep in mind that I would rather be dead than to be a dried-up mistress in His Majesty's court." Gasps of shock and some giggling circulated around the hall and as she held her head high, Anne climbed into her father's carriage and was away to Hever.

January, 1536

Anne and Mary soon reached the chapel. It seemed everyone at court had the same idea as she did. It made her heart smile that Henry had such loyal and loving subjects. She hated to ask for them to leave, but she wanted to be left alone. Knowing her sister's wishes, Mary quietly walked down the side of the pews to where the priest was chanting prayers in Latin. "Please excuse my rudeness, Your Grace, but the queen would like to have the chapel to herself during this time of uncertainty." "Of course, Lady Mary, I will dismiss the congregation so her Majesty can be in prayer." Mary nodded in gratitude and made her way back to Anne, who was secretly hiding behind the opened door to the chapel. She was not hiding from anyone per se, she simply did not know if she had the strength to be confronted with questions she herself did not have the answers to.

"My good Christian people, please take to heart your desire to pray for His Majesty within your quarters and personal chapels. Please continue to pray for the king's quick recovery and for Queen Anne as she, too, prays tirelessly for her husband, the king. Remember, also, to pray for the safety of the unborn prince she now carries, and that this most dramatic event does not cause them any harm. In nomine Patris, et Fillii, et Spiritus Sancti, Amen. Go with God."

Anne could hear everyone whispering in hushed tones and tried to hear what they were saying. When the last person had left the chapel and the halls were nearly clear of anyone who might spot her, Anne quickly made her way into the dimly lit chapel. Since the pomp and circumstance of the Catholic Church was still observed, a multitude of candles had been lit in honor of the king. Everything seemed so uncertain, so dream-like, that before she knew it, she was at the altar making herself comfortable on the velvet cushioned bench that she and Henry had knelt on only hours ago. She looked over her shoulder to see Mary closing the heavy wooden door shut so she could feel truly at peace.

Clasping her hands together, she wanted to begin praying, but Anne felt like she was not being humble enough to speak with God. So she pushed herself away from the bench and slid it over to the side, leaving nothing between herself and the altar. She felt the need to completely give way to her grief. She slowly submitted herself and her body to lie flat on the floor. She brought her hands to rest between her head and the coolness of the stone floor. Now she felt close enough to her humility to finally call upon God.

"Oh, gracious and loving Lord, please have mercy on our anointed king. He is in a poor way and needs your healing to wake him from this slumber that has taken over his wounded body. I beseech you, God, to show pity on my poor husband. I need him more now than ever, since his prince and heir will be born soon enough, granted if it pleases you to bless us. I, too, need your guidance in all matters, while His gracious Majesty is not well, to be able to keep my composure, as it would please him greatly to know I was able to rule in his stead as his one true wife and queen." The tears were rolling down her face, because she knew that even though she was pleading with all her heart, only God could restore the king—if he saw fit to do so.

As she lay silently against the floor, Mary's voice broke the silence of the stifled room. "Anne, Lord

Cromwell is here to see you. Shall I send him away or let him in?"

Anne pondered this for a moment and then softly granted Thomas Cromwell's request. She looked up and turned her head in the direction of the entrance and saw Cromwell quietly slipping through the cracked door. His footsteps were muffled against the floor, no doubt due to the dirt that covered the bottom of his shoes from walking back and forth through the tilt yard. "Lord Cromwell, to what do I owe the pleasure of your hasty visit?" Anne asked sarcastically. Once friends before Anne was crowned queen, he had been a much-valued asset to the Boleyn family. He had been very much in favor to the reformation of the Protestant faith. With the help of Anne and her family, he had been able to make Henry the head of the Church of England after the pope and the Catholic Church had denied granting Henry his annulment.

He had also played a huge roll in passing the Act of Succession in 1534, proclaiming that Catherine and Henry's marriage was seen as null and void in the eyes of God, and that Anne was Henry's one and only true wife and queen. Many people had lost their lands, estates, and even their lives during those tiresome times including Henry's longtime friend and advisor in lawful matters, Sir Thomas Moore. Anne following through with Thomas's had been extremely hard for Henry. There had even been secret talks about secretly banishing Moore to another part of Europe so he could keep his life. But no matter how hard Henry had tried, Thomas's refusal to accept him as Supreme Head of the English Church had made saving his life harder to contemplate.

1535

"Why should I, the King of England, show him mercy just because he has been such a loyal and true friend despite his nonacceptance of what rightfully belongs to me?"

Anne watched her husband struggle within himself day after day with such vigor that she surely thought Thomas may escape a traitor's death. But the position taken by Thomas had remained unchanged, and on the sixth of July 1535, Thomas was brought from the Tower to his place of execution on Tower Hill. Neither Henry nor Anne witnessed his death. One of the priests who had attended Thomas in his final hours reported that everything was done swiftly and accurately, quoting that Moore's last words were, "I die the king's good servant and God's first." Thomas Moore had been only fifty-seven years old, and while Anne, in full support of her husband's wishes, could not help but feel a small sliver of sadness that such a well-respected man should die.

But if Henry had not been so strict with the signing and taking of the oath, the people of England, or Europe, for that matter, would not have recognized Anne as Henry's true and lawful wife. and that any children born to them would be the true heirs to the English throne.

January, 1536

"Lord Cromwell, have you any news of the king, my husband? I beg you to be truthful and forthcoming with everything you know. I may be but a mere woman, but I am your anointed queen, and stronger than most may think I am." Anne managed to slowly rise and walk over to where Cromwell was sitting. He looked so lost and afraid. In one way, she knew exactly how he felt. She also knew that if something were to happen to the king, his future in the English court was very uncertain. The whole of the realm was still reeling with anger and indignation from the dissolution of many cathedrals and churches around England. Even though Henry was now the Supreme Head of the Church of England, many loyal subjects still thought that their faith had been unfairly disrupted by a Protestant reformation backed by Anne herself. While she had doubled the amount of coin and food that she gave to the poor every Sunday as the old queen had, most peasants only believed in the teachings of the Catholic faith.

"Lord Cromwell, I know that we have not seen eye to eye on certain matters for quite some time now, but with the future of the monarchy being unknown or even understood, I do believe that you can do me one favor. I know that behind all the politics and courtly life, you are a simple man with a wife and children. I know that having to be separated from them to serve His Majesty has not been easy or always fair. Know that I, too, have a family, not just with the king but at my home at Hever. I sometimes wish for quieter days and a simple life to be able to enjoy what God has blessed me with. But please, for the love I know you bear for the king, understand that being left in the dark about his situation is something that I cannot manage by myself." Cromwell was staring at her now with an honest and true sincere look of empathy. "I beg you, Master Cromwell, please find a way for me to see my husband. I promise that I will keep all discretion and composure for my unborn child's sake, but grant me this one request. For I know that if it were your wife who was in the gravest of ways, you would do anything to be by her side to provide some soothing words of comfort."

"Your Grace, before I do so, please heed my words. Henry has sustained injuries that are both visible and unknown. He has been unconscious, for the better half of the day, showing no signs of life. Parliament is fearful that things may turn for the worst, and I should advise Your Majesty that the future of England now lies in the stilled hands of our sovereign and the heir you are now carrying. Before coming to chapel, I stopped by His Majesty's chambers where he lies in comfort and in the company of Charles Brandon and his physicians. I must prepare My Lady for what she will see." Anne braced herself for everything that Thomas Cromwell was about to lay out for her. She had never been one to be weak in the knees—or stomach—when it came to injuries.

"His Majesty has significant swelling in his face, arms, and legs. His abdomen is also slightly swollen due to the impact of the horse that crushed him. There are cuts and scrapes all over his skin, and every now and then, a small amount of blood will fall from his nose. He does not look like the robust young king he was this morning." Cromwell closed his swollen eyes and waited to hear Anne's reply. "Thank you, Master Cromwell, you have been more help to me during this horrible time than anyone else, and I will make sure that you are well compensated, either from my privy purse or by the king's own hand, once everything has settled."

Anne, hearing all she needed to hear, stood up and nodded her head at Thomas. "When you think the time is best for me to visit His Majesty, I shall be ready. Merely send word of your plans and I will be obliged to concede to how you wish to proceed." Cromwell nodded in agreement and whispered, "Your Grace," before Anne took her leave back to her chambers.

STEPHANIE BASCO SULLIVAN

Chapter Six

Christmas, 1532

The winter had come quickly and had seemed to cover all of the gardens and roof tops with its pureness. New beginnings, that's what this New Year would bring. Henry and Anne had just gotten back from their hunting expedition across his vast and fruitful lands. They had stayed and held company with many friends and acquaintances Henry had known for many years. They had arrived back to Whitehall Palace just in time for the Christmas festivities. Knowing that Catherine was no longer with in the walls of the palace, Anne had taken it upon herself to adorn the banqueting halls and throne room with anything her heart had desired.

"Oh, Henry, do you really mean it? Decorate any way I see fit?" "Yes, my sweetness. Make everything shine as you are now, and I have no doubt that good tidings of great cheer shall ring all throughout this cold and dreary place." Since Catherine and her ladies had left a few weeks earlier, the servants had been instructed to start engraving his and Anne's initials on every corner of the corridors. Henry had also taken pains to order Catherine's rooms thoroughly cleaned and redecorated with things he knew his new love would be very much surprised by.

Soon every room, banqueting hall or entryway had been adorned by wild holly garlands that had bright red berries scattered throughout the greenery. Anne made sure that taller, brighter candles were placed in every nook and cranny so as to give off a soft glow for the court's pleasure. All the usual holiday favorites were ordered and prepared for Henry and his many guests. Smoked pig and venison aged to perfection. Puddings had been made extra sweet because Henry seemed to have an extra sweet tooth during the holiday season. Liver and minced pies had been placed on each table along with a variety of cheeses and pastries. Pheasant and duck were served sliced and covered in gravy, and each table was adorned by beautiful displays of colorful fruits and nuts for simple snacking.

"Anne, you have truly outdone yourself in planning one of the most elaborate Christmases this palace has ever seen. Everyone will be awestruck by how much you care for their comfort and pleasure." Henry always knew exactly what to say to make her fall even more in love with him.

"Thank you, Your Grace," she replied, "I kept you in mind while I picked everything out. I so want you to be proud of me."

"How could I not be my dearest; you always think of me before yourself, and that, my sweet, is worth more than all the gold in the world."

As all the Nobles and Clergymen began to swarm the halls and look at the splendor that was laid out for their pleasure, nothing took the cake like the announcement of Henry and Anne when they made their grand entrance to the Christmas festivities. Both of them had worn red velvet, trimmed with colorful jewels that resembled a treasure chest. Anne had worn a crown made of holly and berries, to keep in the Christmas theme. Henry looked so dashing in his red velvet tunic and gold crown. His hose showed off his muscular leg tone, and Anne could not help but admire just how dashing her future husband was. She had always thought of him as quite handsome, but never more so than when he doted on her. Several guests requested an audience with the king and while Anne had been more than happy to join in the dancing or welcoming their guests, Henry insisted that she join him in the throne room to receive gifts from his royal subjects.

"Henry, I do not mind staying behind the scenes for the sake of keeping the peace. This is my first time to oversee Christmas plans, and I don't want it to be seen as overstepping my station." In some ways, Anne really could not have cared less what people thought about her presence at court, while the former queen was probably observing the holiday somewhere with all the pomp and circumstance of the Catholic Church. The month before, the couple had secretly married, and now, Henry insisted that Anne stay seated in the chair that had been inhabited by a powerful Spanish princess and English Queen of twenty-four years. But the times were changing, whether the whole of England wanted it to or not, and why not get the English nobility used to seeing her by Henry's side? It was what His Majesty wanted, and she found no good reasons to delay the inevitable.

"I have a gift for you, beautiful Anne." Henry raised one hand and right on cue, two page boys brought in a large, golden chest. Anne stood up and walked down next to the gift.

"Oh, Your Majesty, it's beautiful, and so much detail."

"No, my sweet, the real gift is inside the chest, but I'm glad to see that you're so humble to take delight in receiving a mere golden chest." Henry smiled sweetly at her as he nodded for the lid to be opened. Inside, there were lavish materials of damask, imported silks, and colored cotton.

"Henry, this is too much! These are all so beautiful and extravagant!" She took her time inspecting each fold of fabric, envisioning what she could have made with the bright and beautiful colors.

"Wait until you see what is in the second chest." Anne looked up in complete shock as two more young boys of the court followed suit, opening another golden chest full of much richer fabrics.

"These are for your new bed linens. Every queen should have a bed worthy to receive royalty." Henry proclaimed.

"Thank you, my love, they are beyond what I deserve. I, too, have a very unique gift, which I hope Your Majesty will love just as much." Anne nodded to her brother, George, who brought in two elaborately decorated boar hunting spears. The wood was two-toned, and the intricate engraving was rightfully fit for a king.

Henry jumped up from his throne and grabbed one of the spears from George. He held out the perfectly balanced spear to admire its craftsmanship. "Who made these?" While smiling with excitement, Anne had said, "Master Holbein, of course. Is he not a genius? He said that they are all the rage across Europe, when it comes to having the best." Henry handed the spear to George, and immediately rushing to Anne, picked her up in his arms. After he had given her a well-deserved kiss, he placed her back down.

"My own sweet darling, they are beyond perfect, and perhaps the best gift I have ever received."

Anne fondly remembered the day Henry had provided her with the gift of nobility. "I have a small gift for you. One that will make you more grand than you already are. This will ensure that the entire court can never question your place in my life ever again." Anne could not even have begun to figure out what could possibly be more exquisite than what he had already given her. "Oh, my love, I need nothing more. How could there be anything else that you could possibly bless me with other than the promise of your love?"

"I have chosen to make you Marquess of Pembroke. With this title, your nobility is recognized, and no one can question the validity of our upcoming marriage." Shock had run through her body, because she had known that with this title and position, all her dreams were coming true. Finally, after seven long years, she would be able to plan her wedding to the man of her dreams, the King of England.

1532

On the first of September 1532 Anne was dressed in the finest red velvet gown with gold trim. She bade her ladies braid and pull her long black hair up in a gold laced coverlet lined with pearls. She and four of her chief ladies walked, to the beat of a single drum, to where Henry sat waiting on his throne. Her father and brother, along with her uncle, and Charles Brandon, Henry's closest friend, were in attendance. Anne proceeded to her stopping point, where a silk pillow awaited her. She kneeled on the pillow, and the ceremony began. The patent of creation was read allowed by the Bishop of Winchester, and Henry himself presented her with her coronet. After helping her rise to stand, Henry placed an elaborate Robe of State. After presenting her with her signed and sealed papers, Henry presented his arm for Anne to take. Together, they walked out of the throne room straight to a beautiful banquet that had been prepared for them.

As the two feasted, drank, and danced for hours, Henry surprised her with yet another part to this most distinguished gift. "Anne, we will be leaving for France to visit with King Francis in order to personally get his approval of our marriage."

"Your Majesty, this is all too much. I could never give you a gift as grand as this." Henry gave her a warm smile and leaned in closer to her. When his lips were mere inches from her ear, he whispered, "Oh, my darling, but you will. When you conceive and bear my much-desired son. Then, we can consider our gifts equal, my love." He gently kissed her ear and down her neck.

"My Lord, everyone is beginning to stare." Anne said in protest, even though she would much rather have been in Henry's chambers, alone.

Anne leaned into Henry and whispered in his ear; "Not much longer now my love, not much longer and we shall be free to give in to our deepest desires, and I shall give you a son worthy to be crowned king."

January, 1536

Anne now waited patiently as she could until the clock finally struck eight. Nightfall had come, and while everyone was deep in prayer for their king, the royal guards made sure to keep as many people in their chambers as possible. Just as she was nearly overcome with anxiety, a light knock sounded on her door. Nan cracked open the door, and Thomas Cromwell was waiting on the other side. "Sir Thomas Cromwell is here to see you, Your Majesty." Finally, he had come, but most importantly, he had kept his promise. "Allow him in please, Nan. Ladies, you may be excused; please go and pray for your king." Each lady curtsied and left the room. "Master Cromwell, please come in. Is there any news on my husband, the king?" Anne got up and poured herself a small glass of wine. She offered Cromwell one, as well, and while he usually did not partake, he accepted the glass.

"I have managed to bring one of Henry's robes to conceal your person. Most everyone at court knows that His Majesty is in a critical way, but no one knows exactly how dangerous the situation truly is. The less the people know right now, the better. We will take the back passage in order to keep your visit even more concealed. There is one small matter that I was unable to make possible, Your Grace. Charles Brandon was adamant in staying with the king. He knows that you are coming and has agreed, for the sake of the king and your delicate state, to keep conversation limited and cordial."

"I understand. Thank you, Master Cromwell, you have made me decidedly relieved, considering the circumstances." She placed her empty wine glass down, and with the help of Master Cromwell, slid into Henry's oversized robe, covering her head with the hood. She had made sure to wear a comfortable, loose fitting gown for her visit. She did not know exactly how long she would be away from her rooms, so she planned for a lengthy stay. Thomas lit a candelabra while Anne placed her swollen feet into her slippers. The whole day's events had left her weary. Even though she had rested and propped her feet up after eating very little supper, the few times that she had experienced excruciating abdominal pain had left her exhausted.

"Master Cromwell, if it is all right with you, could we walk slowly? Today has left the prince in a foul way and has made me feel a little anxious."

"As you wish, Your Grace; do I need to summon the physician to attend you once we are in His Majesty's rooms?" His question was genuinely sincere. "Not yet. All I care about is seeing to my husband."

When they arrived at the hidden door that led into Henry's bedchambers, Cromwell stopped short and made sure Anne was truly ready to see her husband. After Anne nodded, he pushed the concealed door open. There, in the middle of his enormous bed, lay her Henry. Charles Brandon stood and bowed as Anne made her way to her husband's bed. Everything around her seemed to fade away like a dream, leaving only her and her beloved in their own private world.

Anne sat down beside the unconscious king, and she began to take in all his external injuries. She reached out and touched Henry's face, leaning in to place a soft kiss on his forehead. It was the only place she felt safe touching, for everywhere she looked, all she saw was black and blue, swollen, or wrapped in cotton cloth. If it were not for his signature red beard, she doubted that anyone, including herself, would have recognized him at all. "Oh, my poor husband, my own darling. I'm somewhat glad that you are not awake to feel the pain that your body is portraying to me now. But I do need you to please push through. I need you, and your son needs you. Elizabeth will need her father when it is time to arrange a royal match for her and her future husband as well as for Lady Mary. Her poor mother was laid to rest today, and I know you have your reasons, but she was not allowed to attend the burial. Know that you are taken down through injury, and I am begging you to look deep within your heart and fight, my love." Tears began to fall down her face. Charles Brandon brought her a handkerchief. "Thank you," she said as his kind gesture caught her off guard.

"Is it all right if we adhere to an informal atmosphere while we are here with our king?" Anne did not see the need to be called Your Majesty, Your Grace, or Your Highness. She was simply Anne, the wife to Henry, and mother to Elizabeth and the future prince. Charles Brandon seemed taken aback for a moment, but readily agreed to Anne's request. "I cannot recall a moment when Henry was so quiet. He always has something to say. Seeing him so helpless has weakened my soul. I've heard from the physicians and Cromwell on how Henry's health is not improving, but tell me, Charles, you have known him your whole life. You know everything about him, even more so than I. What do you think will become of Henry? Is his condition so poor that he will recover with some lasting effects, or will he flounder and succumb to his injuries?"

Her forwardness must have taken Charles by surprise, because he had to sit on the bed, opposite from Anne, of course, in order to convey his thoughts. "Anne, I will not be discrete about Henry's condition. If he were twenty years younger, I might give him a better chance of pulling through. I've seen him get hurt doing stupid and foolish things before, and he always managed to come out of it unscathed. But this time, well, I never have seen Henry thrown so violently off his horse, only to have the heavy animal land on top of him. It was a sight most dreadful, and I wish I could remove every second of it from my memory. When we were able to get him into the medical tent and we removed his armor, I was sure that Henry would come 'round shortly. But after the second hour of seeing nothing, no movement, no signs of life other than his beating heart and slow breathing, I must admit that my hopes began to falter." Charles hung his head low in shame and disgrace, thinking that Anne might find him most unworthy. But to his surprise, she reached over her husband's sleeping body and placed a friendly hand on his. A few tears fell from his face as he responded to her kind gesture.

"No man or king could ask for a better friend, Charles. I know that there has been some bitterness between us these past few years, but in the end, all that truly matters is who is here now." She hoped her words would help Charles see that even though she could be a difficult pill to swallow sometimes, she was not all about ambition. "It must be nice to have such a true and loyal friendship no matter what happens. In the end, having someone by your side is worth more than all the titles and gold in Europe."

STEPHANIE BASCO SULLIVAN

Chapter Seven

1532

The journey to France had been one of great importance for Henry and Anne. After being made Marquess of Pembroke, the king had planned their trip so that the confirmation of his and Anne's marriage could be publicly acknowledged by King Francis. Anne was extremely excited to be going back to French court. "Mary, you must come as one of my ladies. There is nothing keeping you here, and I could use my sister's support." Mary had now been a widow for a couple of years, and Anne thought it high time for her sister to have some fun. She also planned to find her a possible marriage match.

On the evening before they were to set to France, Henry had asked Anne to eat a quiet dinner with him. "I want just the two of us; no guards, no servants, just you and me." Anne agreed, but she quickly reminded him that nothing beyond eating and enjoying each other's company would cross between them. They were so close to being married, and Anne had not wanted to spoil their wedding night. Henry gave her a sly grin, which made her feel a little too excited. "As you wish, my love," Henry had agreed, taking his leave.

All day, Anne's chambers had been full of servants, folding and packing her finest gowns and jewels. She had commissioned new gowns made with the finest fabric, and she could not wait to show them off. She had been so busy making sure everything was just right for their voyage, she came to realize that she had not eaten all day. The little silver clock that sat on her mantle had chimed out seven times, letting Anne know that the king would be expecting her anytime now. "I think we have done all we can do tonight. Please go to your rooms and families. I will not require your assistance tonight. But remember, for those of you who are traveling with the king and myself, be ready on the docks to board first thing tomorrow morning. The ship will depart half past seven, so please don't over indulge yourselves. There is nothing worse than a hung-over crew at sea."

After the last of her ladies had left her rooms, Anne had made herself ready for a restful evening with her love. She had put on her green taffeta gown that had silk trim. She had brushed her long black hair so that it would fall smoothly against her back. Henry loved it when her hair was down. He would run his fingers through it and twirl the ends around his fingers. Placing an emerald band across her head she had given herself a quick glance before leaving for Henry's rooms. When she had arrived at his rooms, the guard opened the door and announced her arrival.

The table had been set for two, with no detail spared. There was a huge roaring fire in the main fireplace, and in every corner of his rooms, there were beautiful candelabras that had been lit for the evening's atmosphere. Anne walked over to the fireplace, and the warmth made her feel extremely relaxed. Even though she had been announced, Henry had been nowhere to be seen. But she had not minded having the silence to herself if only for a moment. Her whole entire life had been about to change, and she had not even stopped to take it all in. Was she really ready to be a queen? Would she be able to produce a healthy male heir that Henry seemed to covet more than her virginity? Would the English people accept her as they had Catherine? So many things had rushed through her head that she had found it almost impossible to focus on simply spending a peaceful night with her sweetheart.

"Anne my darling, I heard you being announced, but I was finishing up on some last-minute paperwork concerning the welfare of my kingdom while we are away." He had made his way to her now, and when he had gotten so close to her that air could not possibly be able to pass between them; he had taken her in his strong arms and kissed her deeply. She could not help but to give way to his fiery and very passionate greeting. Before she knew it, he had begun to explore her mouth more thoroughly with his tongue and she, without hesitation had returned his advances.

"Oh Anne, my one true love, I am becoming ever so impatient with my desire to have all of you. Must we wait for our wedding night? If we are to be married soon, then no one can question any child produced, because we will be husband and wife before the child is born."

"Patience is a virtue, my Lord, but I shall think about what you have proposed." She had given him a loving smile, and Henry had placed her back down on the floor. "Come, I have a great feast prepared for us tonight. In celebration of our upcoming trip and nuptials, a feast befitting a king and his queen." Henry had clapped his hands, and while a few kitchen servants were bringing in the covered silver platters, he had pulled Anne's chair out for her to be seated. Afterwards, he had taken his place at the head of the table.

One by one, each platter had been revealed and left for them to have free range to pick and choose what they wanted. There had been smothered venison and creamed potatoes, liver and kidney pie, sliced ham and turkey, while other platters had assortments of cheeses and fruits to please any palate. Apparently, Henry had forgotten to eat, as well, because he had begun filling his plate with several of the fine foods spread out before them. Anne had quickly followed suit and before they knew it, they had found themselves gorged and quite relaxed by the wine that had been brought to them for refreshment.

Conversation had been very scarce since the feasting had begun. Neither one of them could stop eating long enough to say one word but instead they had simply looked at one another with happiness for a meal well prepared and eagerly devoured.

January, 1536

"Your Majesty, Queen Anne, you must wake up." Anne opened her eyes and saw that the dim light of daybreak was creeping up the east wall of Henry's bedchamber, and there were several of the king's physicians standing around her. Henry, by her side, was lying still. "My Lady, you look exhausted; you have been here all night?" She sat up from her slumped position, and her whole body moaned in protest. "Yes, I have, and please don't lecture me about how unsafe it is for me to be here with my husband. I shall not be going anywhere until I know he is going to recover." If she had a gavel, she would have pounded on the wooded frame of Henry's bed signifying her final and binding decision.

"Your Grace, the king...well, His Majesty has sadly left us to be with our Lord in the very early hours of this morning. We wanted to wake you, but the Duke of Suffolk had insisted that we let you be. But now, the king must be bathed and prepared for burial." Anne straightened herself even more and felt all the blood rush from her head. Then everything went completely dark.

January, 1533

"If you remember my love in your prayers as strongly as I adore you, then I shall be yours forever." - HR

In the very early hours on the twenty-fifth of January, 1533, Anne was roused from her sleep. No one had bothered her or disturbed her in any way, but the uneasy feeling in her stomach left her a little queasy. She jumped quickly out of her warm bed to get to her water basin. She had not been fully convinced that she was with child so soon, but her morning sickness told her otherwise. After she was finished being indisposed, she called on her sister, Mary, to fetch her some fresh water. Mary was very quick to comply, because today was no ordinary day. It was Anne's wedding day.

Anne dipped a strip of linen into the fresh, cool water and began wiping her face and neck. "Are you well, sister?" Mary asked. "Shall I fetch the physician in case you need something for your stomach?"

"No, dear Mary, it is not a stomach illness that stirs in my belly. but your future prince, who has been ever present since we arrived back at court." Mary looked at her with a smile then quickly voiced her concerns.

"Anne, are you certain that you are with child? Does the king know?" Anne could see worry come over Mary's face. She had thought to drag her questions and curiosity out for a little while longer but decided against it. "Mary, everything is well. His Majesty knows that I am pregnant. He guessed it before I ever mentioned that I was having bouts of morning sickness and extreme cravings. We decided to not tell anyone until after our wedding, but you are my sister, and I cannot withhold such a grand secret as this from you."

The two sisters embraced and shed a few happy tears. "How splendid this makes today! My beautiful, raven haired sister is going to marry the King of England, and she is already forthcoming of a prince to please His Majesty." Anne put her finger up to Mary's lips. "Quiet, dearest sister, the king made it abundantly clear not to announce my condition until he does so himself. Promise me you will breathe a word of this to no one, not even our brother George."

"I so swear, Anne. Not one word shall pass through these lips until the announcement has been made. But how far along do you think you may be? We have just returned from France only a month." Mary caught herself before she continued further. "Yes, dear sister, this child was conceived while we were away in France. The physician, who has sworn to secrecy upon pain of death, confirmed the king's suspicions in the early days of November. We had landed in Dover around five in the morning." Anne paused for a moment. She walked over to the thick curtain that separated her bedchamber from the sitting parlor and peaked through a small gap in the fabric to see if anyone else was awake. Nan was walking about, getting a fire started and preparing a bath for Anne to soak in before her wedding.

She quietly walked back over to her sister. "We must not speak any more about this right now. I must make ready for my wedding day." Mary dipped her head in agreement, but her smile stayed constant.

"Daily proof you shall me find, unto you both loving and kind." Anne Boleyn

January, 1536

The darkness consumed her once again, and she knew that her dream had covered her in its mysterious grip. Lately, her dreams had taken her on a whirlwind of memories, and she was quite uncertain as to where this one might take her. She did not know which way to turn or what to do—but as usual, something of the unknown began pulling her towards a dimly lit room. As she proceeded to pass through the opening, she entered into a beautiful, candle-lit room. The sweet and soothing smells of rose petals and lavender filled the air. The bedchamber was elaborately decorated, and she could easily tell whose rooms she had entered,

Henry's. They were his lodgings at Dover, where they had stayed for almost a month before returning to court at Etham Palace.

1532

The journey to France had been long and tiresome. While some of Henry's requests had been met, others had not. King Francis I was a most gracious host. He provided entertainment and banquets displaying all that France had to offer to show his support for Henry's marriage to Anne. Once they arrived, the fanfare that gathered to welcome the couple was quite lavish. As the two monarchs met face to face and embraced as if brothers, Anne was treated like any woman of royal birth. Looking around the room, Anne noticed that Queen Claude was not in attendance. She wanted to see her so much and to show her that her education in France had not been for just any marriage, but a marriage to a king. "Ah, LaBelle Anne," King Francis said, bowing with acknowledgement. "I am so very sorry that my wife, Queen Claude, could not attend. She was feeling under the weather and thought it best to not be at court." Anne knew perfectly well why the queen had not attended her arrival. She did not approve of Henry's choice in a bride. But while she allowed speculation to run through her mind, she made sure not to let it show.

"Not to worry, Your Grace, I hope all is well with her soon." They began their visit with a full banquet. The eating, drinking, and dancing ran long into the night.

1536

Then it hit Anne as she realized the scene now unfolding was that of the night that Henry had asked her, once again, to dine with him. Anxiously awaiting their secret wedding ceremony, which had been arranged to take place at Whitehall, the two lovers had decided that an evening to themselves would be exactly what they needed. Anne's loins ached with desire and excitement.

1532

Neither of them was extremely hungry, so a large silver tray was loaded with cheese, grapes, strawberries, and sweet rolls as well as raspberry tarts, one of Henry's favorites. Two vessels of wine were brought in as well, so that after the door was closed on their private picnic, no one would need to be summoned again that night. Knowing that their wedding would take place within a few months, Anne had decided to wear a rather revealing night gown that was covered with a green velvet evening robe to keep her from freezing. Henry, too, had seen fit to wear his pants and a white cotton shirt for comfort. He had left the shirt untied so Anne could see his auburn chest hair. She had often commented on how handsome he looked with his trim cut chest that showed just how strong and athletic he was.

The evening began with eating some of the foods that had been brought up for them, followed by conversations about their trip to France. "Are you happy my dearest? The King of France has gladly recognized our union and soon you shall be crowned Queen of England." Henry beamed with pride while he waited on his future bride to respond. Anne knew that she and Henry would be married and that he wanted her so badly that he had moved Heaven and Earth to get her, but she was not so sure that the people of England felt as receptive to her as they had their other queen. Tread lightly, Anne, do not dampen or spoil this most perfect night.

"Yes, my love, I am overwhelmed at how nice everyone has been since your decision to take me as your true wife. I suppose I'm just a little nervous, that's all, nothing to worry yourself about. Mother says that every bride has insecurities right before her wedding day. It's practically expected, and since ours is not going to be the lavish ceremony that I had envisioned, I have no doubt that our small ceremony will be just as special." She made sure to give Henry a sincere smile to keep from alarming him. She had hoped with all her heart that she would be received by Queen Claude while they were in France. She had thought of the beautiful queen as her friend and ally. But when King Francis said that she was unwell and unable to attend court while she and Henry were present, Anne feeling rather injured.

"Anne, there is nothing to be apprehensive about. The people love you as much as I do, and they will accept you as my wife and queen. And for those that do not, they will soon have to force my hand in making them see things my way or suffer the consequences." Henry, very pleased with himself, popped a grape into his mouth and sat back in his chair, giving Anne a come-hither stare. Without him having to ask, Anne pushed back her chair and slowly stood up. She seductively untied and the ribbons on her green velvet robe, keeping full eye contact with Henry. She wanted to entice him, and by the look on his face, she was succeeding. She let the heavy garment fall to the floor and with the fire to her back; she knew that the fire light would cast a light through her thin cotton nightgown, showing Henry her every curve.

Seeing that his interest had been achieved, she walked slowly towards him, stopping every few steps to pull at one of the strings that kept her night dress on. Henry shifted in anticipation of her final destination, and soon he was granted his surprise. Anne slowly stopped in front of him, staring deep into his hungry eyes. She felt the need to straddle him in the chair and kiss him ever so passionately in order to cool her own desires. Henry met her kiss with enthusiasm and greediness. After a lustful kiss, Henry began kissing her neck tenderly, and Anne rolled her head back to allow him access to her bare skin. One sleeve of her night gown had slid slightly off her shoulder, and Henry seized the opportunity to consume that part of her, as well.

Anne let out a slight gasp as Henry found and exposed her breasts. He wasted no time in partaking of her half- nakedness. His tongue rounded each breast with his consuming passions, and as Anne arched her back in response to his exploration of her, she leaned backwards until Henry's strong and wanting arms grabbed her from getting away. She opened her eyes and saw a fire so intense in Henry's eyes that all she wanted was to rip off his shirt and see his magnificent body. So with one firm pull in either direction, Anne managed to rip Henry's shirt completely in two. This must have pleased him greatly, because as she leaned in to kiss his chest, he let out a moan of passion. "Oh, my buxom lady, my love, I have waited so long to see your body. I must see more of it, for if I don't, I think I shall surely die a wanting man."

By now, Anne could feel his manhood beneath her nightgown, and her natural lust for him overtook her. She craved him with such a hunger that the only way she could find release was to give in to both their desires. Henry scooped her up in a matter of seconds and carried her over to his bed. He laid her down gently, and before her back settled against the fur lined bed, Henry pulled her gown completely off exposing her naked body.

"Anne, you are so beautiful and much desired. I am overwhelmed with passion and I hope to concede to your every desire while you are in my arms. The firelight left a soft glow on her naked body which made Henry crave her even more. "Are you sure, my darling? It is not our true wedding night, and I do not want to rush against your wishes." He was so sincere with her concerns that it made her want him even more. "Come, my love, let us join our hearts, souls and bodies to set in motion what is to come. Lie with me, and together, we will conceive your son."

Henry removed the rest of his clothing, revealing his entire body to her. He was magnificently sculpted. His wanting of her had fully revealed itself, and he slowly climbed into bed beside her. He was found wanting every inch of her body and made sure to not just touch her smooth skin, but follow it with a soft kiss. When his fingers found the mound between her legs, he moaned in approval at how ready she was to receive him. He pulled himself on top of her and kissed her passionately. He pulled one of her legs up beside him and slowly entered her. Anne cried out, but only a little…. He entered her a few more times, and Anne's body responded to his until they both reached their ecstasy.

January, 1536

"Your Majesty, are you all right?" Madge was lightly shaking Anne to rouse her from what she thought might be a terrible nightmare. Anne could hear her cousin's voice but could not seem to find her way out of her dream. Mary was now wiping her sister's face with a cool wet cloth in hopes of rousing her. After a couple of pats, Anne began to rouse. The room was completely dark, save flickers from fire roaring in her fireplace. Wait—her fireplace—how did she get here? Where was Henry? "Mary, dear sister, what is going on? The last I remember, I was sitting with the king and the Duke of Suffolk talking about how strong and resilient the king is. Oh Mary, Henry, how is my Henry?"

The mood in the room was silent as the night. Each of her ladies seemed busy with something in order to not come across the queen. Anne looked around for someone to respond, but not a single face could manage to look at hers. Finally, Anne grabbed her sister's arm. "Mary, for the love of God, what has happened? I demand to know what is going on with my husband. Am I not the Queen of England?" Hot tears gathered in the corners of her eyes. "My patience is wearing thin, and I need to know exactly what is going on. I will not ask again." Just before Anne's sister could begin telling her everything that transpired, Thomas Cromwell was announced, and he was shown into Anne's bedchambers. He had his hat in his hands and a very sad demeanor about his person. "Your Majesty, it is with my deepest regret to report to you that His Majesty, Henry VIII, has succumbed to the injuries that he suffered during the jousting accident yesterday. You and Charles Brandon were at his bedside while he was still with us, but sometime during the night, he entered into the arms of our Heavenly Father. You had fallen asleep holding his hand, and when we woke you this morning with the news, the shock of it all left you in such sorts that Mr. Brandon insisted that we bring you to your chambers for the sake of your unborn child."

Anne had no memory of anything that had taken place since she had drifted off to sleep at Henry's side the night before.

The words seemed to echo and repeat rapidly inside her head. *Dead, my Henry is dead? No, how can this be true? He was merely resting when I saw him last. I saw him breathing—I saw him with my own eyes.*

Panic began to feed her emotions very quickly, and she felt as though she could faint at any second. "Where is my daughter, Elizabeth? I must have her here with me—and my father. Yes, my father can make this all better. Send for them quickly." Anne did not want anyone to see her lose her composure, so she asked for everyone aside from her sister to leave her chambers. Each lady curtsied and left Anne's sight. Thomas Cromwell lingered for a moment more until all the ladies were out of the rooms. "Master Cromwell, I don't mean any disrespect, but please, just leave me with all that you have reported so that I may have plenty of time to process it all."

"Your Majesty, I just wanted to pass on my deepest sympathy and to let you know that the Privy Council has come to session to discuss the proceedings of announcing His Majesty's untimely passing and for planning his funeral. Know that all things will be made known to you before the final preparations are made. The matters of state are being discussed as we sit here now, and I will convey your instructions on how you would like for everything to proceed. After you have had some time to process everything." He dipped down on one knee and bowed his head.

"Thank you, Master Cromwell. You have been most gracious and kind to me, and for that I will always be grateful. When you have a summary of all the things I need to look over, please bring them to me."

Cromwell stood up and paused for a second before disappearing from her sight. There was a constant dull ache in her belly, and she did not know if it was from the news of Henry's passing or her unborn child showing his distaste for all that had happened in only a short time. What was going to happen to her now? What about her daughter, Elizabeth? Oh God, what about Catherine's daughter, the Lady Mary? Was Mary going to pose a problem now that her father was no longer here to keep her in check by his command? *Will the Catholic Church see this as an opportunity to place her on the throne and banish her, Elizabeth and her unborn son? Oh Henry, I told you that I did not like your being so careless with your need to be the best at everything. Why did he have to die now? Why has he left me so helpless and alone with people that never wanted me to be their queen in the first place?*

All she could do was wait—wait for her father to provide some comfort and guidance. Wait for her very young daughter—and heir to the throne—to be brought to her so she could be with the only part of Henry she had left. Her unborn child would be left in a limbo of uncertainty until he was born. Everything depended on the safe and healthy delivery of Henry's son. Time had become a weight that constricted her and a constant companion to which she was not ready to concede. She had been taught from childhood that patience was a virtue. But now that it seemed a period of endless waiting was staring her in the face, she wanted absolutely nothing to do with it or the impending manner in which she should conduct herself.

Chapter Eight

While Anne waited in her sitting room for her father to arrive, memories of her wedding day came to mind. She had hoped for a very lavish ceremony befitting the future Queen of England. She had remembered reading the accounts of Henry's marriage to Catherine and wondered—if they were now considered divorced, why could she not have the same glamour and respect that the former queen had received for both her ceremonies? Even though it had been a private ceremony in which there were few attendants, Catherine had still worn a lavish off-white gown that was ornately decorated with jewels. Then, just twelve days later, both Henry and Catherine had been crowned together at Westminster, finally and formally, uniting England and Spain.

January, 1533

"Aren't all weddings supposed to be elaborate and well celebrated?" Henry and Anne had already wed in a private ceremony the November prior, and now, even though secret, Anne had hoped for more pomp and circumstance. But Henry had said that, given the circumstances surrounding his break with the Catholic

Church and becoming Head of the Church of England, they would need to keep the marriage a secret for the time being. There were still many supporters of Catherine who would have loved the chance to displace Anne if given the chance, and since Anne had now been carrying the king's child, their marriage would establish that child as his heir. Anne's sister, Mary, had come to help bathe and dress her for her wedding day. Mary and their brother, George, would act as witnesses. Their father and the Duke of Suffolk would also be in attendance. The wedding would take place in a chamber above the Holbein Gate. "Here it is," Mary said cheerfully. She pulled a silver damask gown trimmed in diamonds and pearls. The front panel of the gown was made of imported silk that had tiny pearls sewn all over the fabric. The bodice was designed in the French fashion, with a square cut. Larger pearls and small clear diamonds outlined the top of the bodice, which had enhanced Anne's slightly bulging breasts. The sleeves had been tied on by silver ribbons and remained simple, so as not to take away from the rest of the gown. A small train had finished off the beautifully made garment. Once Mary and Nan laced up the gown and placed a small diamond tiara upon her black hair that had been braided and pulled up, Anne was ready.

"Oh sister, you are a vision to behold. A true Queen of England. His Majesty will be most pleased." Mary said. Mary gave her nervous sister a hug before they headed into the adjoining rooms in which Henry had been waiting to make Anne his wife. Mary and Nan had picked some flowers from the surrounding gardens to hang across the altar, and they had made Anne a simple bouquet to ward off bad luck. When the doors to the room opened, four choir boys began singing a beautiful hymn in Latin. With a nod from Henry, Anne's father came to her side and offered his hand for her to take. "What a most happy day it is, my darling daughter; my golden Anne. You look like a queen already." She gave her father a quick smile, and with one foot in front of the other, they came to stand before the handsome king. Anne looked up at Henry, who had been staring straight ahead.

"Good morning my love," Anne whispered, hoping that he would look at her and compliment her wedding attire, but he did not. Henry remained ever-concentrated on the task at hand. A small twinge of sadness seared through her heart. She had been certain that Henry would have at least acknowledged her appearance on their wedding day, commenting how beautiful—or how ugly—he thought her to be. Either remark would have been better than the cold reception he provided.

"We are gathered here in the sight of God and these few witnesses to join His Majesty, King Henry VIII of England, to Anne Boleyn, the Marquess of Pembroke, in the holy bonds of marriage. We ask those here if there are any reasons as to why these two should not be joined in the eyes of God to come forth or forever hold their tongues." The reading of the banns concluded, Archbishop Cranmer paused for only a second before telling the couple to join hands. "Do you, Henry, take Anne to be your wife, forsaking all others until God calls you from this world?" Henry replied with a commanding and stern "I do," then Cranmer turned to Anne. "Do you, Anne, take Henry to be your rightful husband, to be bonny and buxom in bed and at the board, forsaking all others, until God calls you from this World?" "I do," she replied in the same monotoned voice as Henry had used just moments before. "Your Majesty, please place the ring that you have chosen to signify your marriage to this woman on her left hand." Henry turned to Charles Brandon, who placed a gold band, adorned with a single ruby, into the king's open hand. Henry then turned to Anne, and for the first time, he actually looked at her.

His face finally lit up with a very happy smile. *There's my Henry.* His eyes never left hers as he slid the ring onto her bare hand. After the ring was securely in its place, Henry slowly looked his bride over from top to bottom. He must have been very pleased with how she looked, because Archbishop Cranmer had to repeat "You may now seal your marriage with a kiss." Both bride and groom let out a little giggle, and with one swift move, Henry pulled Anne close to him, bending down to kiss her.

After a few moments, someone in the room cleared their throat, which brought the lovers out of their embrace. A flood of congratulations filled the room, and the small wedding party proceeded to a banquet that would serve as their wedding feast.

January, 1536

"The Earl of Wiltshire, Your Majesty." Nan announced and brought Anne back to the present. She waited for the curtain to be drawn before she started crying. Her father walked over to her and knelt down beside her. "Anne, my poor daughter, I do not have the words to bring you comfort. I have searched high and low for some reasoning for what has transpired but to no avail. I have found none. How is the child within your belly? No signs of distress, I hope. We do not need any further misfortunes to fall upon us this day."

Anne looked up at her father, who had by now stood up and walked to the window. "No further misfortunes upon us? Are you completely mad or just inconsiderate? To whose misfortunes are you referring, dear Father? Certainly not mine, for as you can plainly see, I am still with child, and soon my daughter, princess Elizabeth, will be here. And until this child I carry is safely delivered and announced as the sole heir to the Tudor throne, I will not have negative talk about our position here at court." A slight discomfort passed through her belly, and she rubbed her hands across her aching bump.

"My husband is dead. The fate of my security on the English throne has been put into a state of uncertainty until either I have Henry's son or Elizabeth comes of age. The Privy Council has been meeting without me, and the only thing that ensures my daughter's protection, and mine, against the Lady Mary and Rome is the Act of Succession. The whole of London is predominately Catholic and if they see their chance, they will raise an army twice the size of Spain's and rid themselves of their Protestant queen and her daughter."

"Anne, calm yourself, yes, the council has been meeting, but not behind your back. You have been indisposed and in no condition to attend such matters. Your brother, George, and I have made it completely clear that anyone caught relaying any messages to or from the Lady Mary or the pope is considered a traitor. The only discussion at hand is that of the king's funeral preparations."

"Funeral preparations, this cannot be happening. I cannot be a widow. My children cannot be fatherless. Elizabeth is only four months old. She's far too young to be without her father. I cannot go through another pregnancy or child birth knowing Henry will not be waiting eagerly for news of my success."

"My dear daughter, all will be well. Cromwell has been gathering all papers needed to show your security on the throne as Queen Regent for Elizabeth until she reaches the age of seventeen, or if you, by God's grace, give us a prince, you will still be regent until your son is of the proper age to rule. The king was no fool. He had already drawn up his will and revised it after the two of you were married. A wise king is always looking forward in his investments." Anne knew that her father was only trying to say uplifting things to help reassure her, but all she could think about was her poor husband. As her father continued on, Anne remembered fonder times as she thought about her coronation.

June, 1533

It had been a rather warm and sunny day in June. Henry had chosen the 1st, which was a Sunday, to be set aside for Anne's grand coronation. Anne had been in her fifth month of pregnancy, and the entire kingdom had been busy with preparations for the

104

event. Anne had never felt better than she did on this day. Excitement seemed to suit her, because Henry could not keep his hands off her. "How are my two most precious jewels this morning?"

"We are well, Your Grace. Though I must admit that I am a little nervous, I believe it is only natural. I just want the people to be happy with me as your queen. Not many were excited to know that we had secretly married. I felt like we were hiding it for the sake of keeping peace instead of celebrating our union." Henry reached for her hand and kissed it softly. "Anne, you must not let the idle talk of common people enter your pretty little head. People don't like change. It's not in their nature to recognize it at first. But they will love you, because they love me." Anne smiled and wanted to say more but Henry had quickly dismissed her. "Now, go make yourself ready. For today is the day you truly become my queen. Just remember, one foot in front of the other until you are beside me. Then the rest will fall in to place. Afterwards, there is to be a great banquet in your honor. The largest feast you have ever seen and the finest people there to greet you, as not my wife, but my queen." He had gave her an even larger smile before bowing and walking away.

Anne was led from the Palace of Westminster to Westminster Abbey, dressed in a purple gown and a robe of gold cloth, decorated with jewels. there were sixty young ladies who walked behind her, carrying her long train. She had been quite nervous while the ladies had been getting her ready, but as soon as she arrived at the Abbey, something inside her made her feel like this was exactly where she was supposed to be. The doors opened, and she walked down the long aisle, which had been blanketed by a red carpet. A choir sang out with such clarity and harmony that she was sure all of Europe could hear them. It made her unborn child move quickly in her belly but she dared not acknowledge it.

When she made it to the High Altar, she prostrated herself before receiving the Crown of St. Edwards and the rod and scepter from the Archbishop of Canterbury. Henry was seated to her left, and he, too, was dressed in similar fashion and colors. The words, "Long live the king, long live the queen," was shouted after Anne took her place beside Henry, and with smiles upon both their faces, they proceeded to retire in order to change their clothing and join all of English nobility for the celebration feasts. It was truly a day to remember, for memories were all she had now.

Chapter Nine

January,1536

It was raining again, and it showed no signs of stopping. How befitting, though; the ill weather merely reflected how Anne felt on the inside. *How could Henry be gone?* Elizabeth snuggled closer to her for warmth on this cold and dreary day. She remembered how long it had taken for Catherine of Aragon to finally be laid to rest. Twenty-two long days of preparations and masses—for a short time, Anne had thought that the whole country would go into mourning over this one woman. True, she had been wife and queen to the King of England, but she had not given the king what he had desired and asked of her: a son. The late queen had once given Henry a son, but the poor thing had lived only fifty-two days.

She remembered hearing the news in France and thinking how sad it must have been for both the king and the queen. She had once seen Queen Claude give birth to a stillborn daughter. The whole kingdom had continued like nothing had happened, but behind closed doors, queen Claude had been beside herself with grief. Anne had thought it rather cold and rude how no one had seemed to care how the queen had felt. Of course, girls were not considered good fortune when it came to Royalty, but still, how heartless can some people be?

February, 1536

Henry's death had finally been announced to the people after Elizabeth had been brought to court and the Lady Mary had been safely relocated to a secret palace. This was done for the safety of Anne, Elizabeth, and the unborn child that had yet made his arrival. The plans had taken almost a month, and now Anne was in the latter part of her fourth month of pregnancy. No autopsy had been performed, at the request of Anne. She could not bear the thought of Henry being cut on, dead or alive. "What's done is done," she said to Cromwell when the question arose. The subjects of how long the king's body would lie in state, and when and where Henry might be laid to rest, were all anyone could talk about.

Anne had been appointed Queen Regent to Princess Elizabeth and had been given Henry's seat amongst the Privy Council. She did not mind tending to the affairs of State, but being here in Henry's chair simply did not feel right. "Gentlemen, if I might suggest, the king will be laid to rest two days from now in St. George's Chapel in Windsor. At which time, our daughter, the Princess Elizabeth, will be proclaimed Queen of England upon turning the age of seventeen. The people will wonder if the child I carry will affect the order of succession, so I propose this announcement according to the Act of Succession: if I deliver a son, he will become the heir apparent before Elizabeth. If God sees fit for me to have another daughter, then she will be second in line *after* Elizabeth. The fact remains that Mary, being His Majesty's legitimate daughter, *in the eyes of the Catholic Church,* must remain hidden and all ties cut from the pope. She is twenty years old, and with over half of the country staying true to their Catholic religion, we could see uprisings. This is something that we cannot afford to happen. England cannot financially withstand a war against Rome. The sooner we name Henry's successor, the better."

Most of the Council agreed with Anne, but there were still a few that had way too much ambition in their eyes. She planned to invest in removing them from court as soon as possible. Thomas Cromwell had become a little softer around the edges with a little girl around the palace. Anne was not accepting the leaving of her daughter alone with just any nursery maids. The next few days were very crucial, and no one could be trusted. Elizabeth was watched after by Mary, George, or their father. Anne did not even trust her uncle, the Duke of Norfolk, with the security of her daughter's life. Even though he was family, he still had an ambitious nature, which could be very dangerous in times like these.

The Duke of Norfolk was a cunning man. He had been brought up to deal in matters of politics concerning the Tudor court. Henry had entrusted him with many things during his lifetime, Anne being one of them. Anne had very little to do with her uncle, until he had come hunting a distraction for the king when Catherine had miscarried yet another child. He had seen the potential of having two beautiful nieces to place in the king's path—and possibly his bed—so naturally, that would raise their family up in the scheme of things. Poor Mary was the first target to be sighted. Even though she had just been married, their uncle knew that Mary had not only been at French court, but that she had bedded King Francis as well.

Anne's sister was a fair, petite young woman with long, blonde hair. Like Anne, Mary had been taught how to speak French and Latin. She had an average singing voice but liked to play the lute. She excelled in writing letters, embroidery, and reciting poetry. Queen Claude had expected all her ladies to be educated. When their uncle heard that Henry was growing weary and frustrated with Queen Catherine, Mary had quickly been placed in his presence. Anne had always thought it unwise for a married woman to bed another man, but their uncle had insisted that Mary's husband, William Stafford, would accept his new position at court and commend his wife to the king's bed.

Anne remembered a heated discussion that had involved Mary, William, both parents, and their uncle. It had taken place the night before Mary was to be taken to court to become one of Catherine's ladies.

1522

"But Thomas, she's already married. You arranged the union yourself, saying that it was a fine match for her. Now you want to whore her out to the King of England just because His Majesty is unhappy? Dear brother, have you no shame, no sense of pride or decorum? She is your own flesh and blood, yet you want her to become the king's mistress?" Their mother was furious and was not willing to just sit by while the future of her children was decided by one ambitious and greedy man.

"Sister, I highly urge you to hold your tongue. This is a conversation, between men, that concerns the king. Not business for a woman."

"I'm not just a woman, dear brother; I am their mother and a Christian woman who believes in the sanctity of marriage, or does going to hell for encouraging adultery not frighten you?"

"The king has asked about Mary, and I intend on giving him what he desires at any cost. I am merely His Majesty's humble servant."

"You are his whipping boy, and you will reap what you sow if you continue on this path. Thomas Boleyn, you had better look deep within yourself before you sell your soul to the devil for advancement. I wash my hands of you, dear brother. I only wish you had daughters, so that you could whore them out for your advancements instead of mine."

"That is all, sister, you may leave us now. Clearly, this is why men do the king's bidding. The weaker sex would shut down a kingdom for the sake of their virginity." Anne heard her mother huff in distaste and leave the room, making sure to slam the heavy wooden door behind her. Anne continued to listen to the conversation at hand. "Since the king has asked for Mary personally, she will be given the highest station within the queen's household. William, in order to ensure that there will be no jealousy, His Majesty has assigned you a mission in France. You may be detained there for a while, so enjoy your freedom as you once did before marrying my niece. Now, say your goodbyes to your wife, and off with you. There is much to be discussed with Mary, and you need not be present."

William walked over to his wife, and with his bowed head, could only manage to close his eyes and kiss his wife on the forehead before leaving. Anne could hear her sister crying once the door was shut, and in true fashion, their uncle took charge. "Sweet niece, do you know what has been bestowed upon you? The position, the possibilities, the wealth and status? If you were to give the king a son, His Majesty would most likely recognize him, and a Boleyn could one day be King of England."

"Is that all you take me for, Uncle, a breeding mare? Doesn't the king have women he can bed other than me?" Mary started sobbing again.

"You will go, you will be presented to the king, and you will do whatever he wishes. Is that clear, or do I have to beat it into you? Think of your family, not just yourself."

1536

"Anne, are you all right?" Mary asked, bringing her back into the present once again. "Yes, I'm fine. I was just thinking of days long gone. When things were simple and yet not so simple, if that makes any sense."

"You are under a lot of stress right now. You've lost your husband, your daughter has become first in line to the throne, and you are carrying yet another child. Honestly, I don't know how on earth you manage it. You truly are a queen." Mary gave her a much-needed embrace. "Mary, do you ever regret how we came to be where we are now? I mean, it was not what you wanted, but you did your duty despite what others thought about you. And you stayed with me throughout my entire courtship with the king until Catherine was sent away. Yet, here you are, still loving and loyal as ever. Does it ever bother you that we were used as pawns in this game of life?"

"My sweet sister, you are the strongest person I know. Even though you are younger than I, you are definitely the wiser. You did something that most women in this court would never dream of doing. You captured and held a king's love for seven years without submitting yourself completely. You showed Henry that the Catholic Church was not in charge of this kingdom and its affairs. You achieved your station by earning his trust and his love, not by giving yourself to him as I did, but by educating him in being a better king, and he realized that. Mother would have been proud of how you handled yourself these past ten years, that I have no doubt. And now, how you still push forward, even during your darkest hours, you exude nothing but calmness and strength, as any ruler would."

"Thank you, Mary. I am beyond grateful that you are here. I know that you would much rather be at your country estate with your husband and children, but you have braved the storm once again and stuck by my side. I love you for that."

"I love you, too, dear sister" Mary replied.

During the daytime, the grief was not as bad, but when the sun had set and everything was settled for the night, Anne missed Henry the most. When she was not with child, Henry had come to her rooms every night. Sometimes, they would play cards or Henry would play a new song on the lute that he had composed earlier that day. Other times, it would be nothing but constant lovemaking that had passed between them until the candles would burn out. She loved how he had craved her. Sometimes, if something had upset him in a council meeting, he would send for her, and they would go horseback riding or hunting, depending on his mood. On rare occasions, just the two of them would go riding about the countryside, finding a beautiful patch of grass beside a stream, where they would make love for hours until starvation had beckoned them back to the palace. Henry had always been a very passionate lover. She had never known that sex could be so intoxicating until she had given in to Henry's pleas. It had not been long until she, too, had found herself wanting of Henry's body on hers. But now, there would be no more midnight lovemaking, no playing cards, and no drinking wine until the sun came up—or sneaking off to enjoy the wonders of nature. She missed his smile, the sound of his voice, and when he laughed so hard he gasped for breath. She missed his smell—that manly, outside musk that seemed to captivate her senses.

Elizabeth had started sleeping in her bed. Anne did not mind, when she needed to, she could roll over and wrap her arms around her tiny daughter and hold her until she fell asleep. Elizabeth was every bit her father, made over, from her flaming red hair to her fiery temper when she did not get her way. Anne knew there were bits and pieces of her mixed in there as well, but for the most part, Henry Tudor had marked his daughter well. She would make sure that Elizabeth would receive an education suited for a future queen, and when the time came to find her a husband, she would make sure he was worthy of Henry VIII's daughter. But for now, Anne wanted Elizabeth to stay tiny, so she could keep her close little bit longer. Anne had been forced to let go of her beloved Henry, but she did not intend to let go of their daughter anytime soon.

Chapter Ten

"O Death, rock me to sleep, bring me to quiet rest, let pass my weary guiltless ghost out of my careful breast. And thus I take my leave of this world." - Anne Boleyn, The Tudors

February, 1536

Anne woke early to the sounds of thunder rumbling through the sky. The day had finally come, and she was not going to move from her bed until she was forced to. The pounding the thunder must have stirred the babe inside her womb, because her belly rolled with movements. "Hello sweet prince," she said, rubbing her belly. She felt a strong kick and laughed a little. "My goodness, you are very active this morning. I wish your father were here to feel you move. He was patiently waiting for you to be born. I may have to call you Harry if your hair is as red as your sisters."

"Good morning, Your Grace. How are you feeling this morning?" Nan asked, wiping the sleep from her eyes. She stopped short, realizing that today was the day the king would be laid to rest. "Please forgive me, Your Majesty. I had forgotten myself. I beg your forgiveness."

"Nan, please don't be sorry. I'm trying my hardest not to break completely down until I can hold it back no longer. Has my black gown arrived yet? What about Elizabeth's?"

"All is well and taken care of, Your Grace. All will be well."

"Nan, what about the Lady Mary? Has word been sent to her about when she may attend her father's funeral?" Most people wanted to make Anne out to be a monster with a cold heart, but she had no reason to deny Mary a final goodbye to her own father. After all, Anne had not particularly cared for the way Henry had handled things when Catherine had died. She understood why he had had denied them visitation while the former queen was still living. The two women, together, would have brought down the whole British monarchy with the snap of a finger if they had been granted to see one another, but when death had separated mother and child, Mary should have been allowed to at least attend her mother's burial.

January, 1536

Catherine of Aragon, the great Spanish princess, the daughter of two of the greatest rulers in Spain, had succumbed to her death bed the seventh of January, 1536. She was fifty years old and considered to be of a fine age of her life. Henry and Anne had been coming out from under the heaviness of a recent miscarriage, but were hopeful that Anne was with child once again, when they had received the news of Catherine's death. In her final hours, the Dowager princess, as was her title known throughout the court, had her last words and testament written with the instructions to delivery to Henry upon her death. When the letter arrived, Anne asked Henry if he wanted to be alone and he solemnly answered, "No, my love. Will you be kind hearted and stay as I read Catherine's final words?"

Anne nodded and sat down in a chair across from Henry. *No matter what is said in the contents of this letter, show no change in your face.* Henry slowly unfolded the paper and began to read:

"My most dear king and husband,

"The hour of my death now drawing on, the tender love I owe you forceth me, my case being such, to commend myself to you. For my part, I pardon you everything and I wish to devoutly pray God that He will pardon you everything. For the rest, I commend unto you our daughter Mary, beseeching you to be a good father unto her, as I have desired. Lastly, I make this vow, that mine eyes desire you above all things.

"Catherine the Queen"

After Henry finished reading the letter, there was a long period of silence. Even though their marriage was officially over, and Henry was now truly free from the hold Catherine seemed to have on him even though they were no longer husband and wife, Anne still sensed that there was a mutual love and respect that Henry still had for his first wife and queen. After all, how can you be with someone for twenty-four years, suffer the loss of several children only to have one child survive, and not feel some extreme loss? Most people at court wanted to make Anne out to be the true reason for Henry's break with his former wife and queen, but idle gossip had only fueled Henry's desire for her all the more. "Henry, it's all right to feel sadness for the passing of Catherine; it is only natural and, most likely, expected. After all, twenty-four years is a long time, and you do have Mary to think about. You do not have to mourn outside these rooms if you so desire, but trust that I will not think ill of you if you need some time to gather yourself.

"Oh, my sweet Anne, you know me all too well. Even though I was only a child when Catherine arrived from Spain to marry my brother, Arthur, you can imagine how taken I was with her; a beautiful foreign princess that I had heard about since I was old enough to understand my older brother's role. I was just excited to be a part of the festivities. My Lady Grandmother had gone with me abroad to visit holy sites and to pay homage to several saints before Catherine's arrival. I was not educated in becoming a king; instead, it was decided that after Arthur and Catherine were married, I would travel more to prepare myself for a life dedicated to the church.

To speak plainly, I never wanted to become a man of the cloth. I much preferred the freedoms and possibilities of courtly life to that of serving God. My mother understood this, but Lady Grandmother had a very difficult time understanding my wishes."

"Was she not concerned about any possibilities that if something were to go wrong and Arthur, God rest his soul, could not perform his royal obligations that another prince would need to take his place? That's why kings and queens have as many children as they possibly can in hopes of producing several male heirs." Anne recalled hearing stories of Henry being referred to as the spare and had always thought it rather ridiculous that the second prince be known as such. "That did not bother me. However, Arthur had never really been one to delve into politics. He was always falling ill with something that the physicians were unsure of and unable to find a cure for. I called him 'fairly Arthur' behind closed doors." Henry let out a small chuckle. "You know, our father would have us both in the gardens practicing our sword fighting, and while I was five years younger than Arthur, I could lift the sword my father had carried during the Battle of Bosworth when he secured the crown from Richard the Third. Arthur, try as he might, could never fully hold the sword like I could. Call it brother's intuition, but sometimes, I just felt it in my bones that my brother would not become king. Is that horrible of me to say of my poor, departed brother?"

"Not at all, my love; you had a vision for yourself, and for England, and when the time came, you did what you thought was right in the eyes of God and for the greater good of your kingdom. Catherine was very lucky to have had you, as both a brother and a husband. Not just any ordinary king would take in his brother's widow and place a crown on her head. But you saw past any indiscretions that Arthur and Catherine might have shared as husband and wife, and gave her peace of mind and a loving marriage. It was not your fault that she could not give you a son. It was only when you searched your heart and soul that you finally realized that she had deceived you for her own advancement. Never apologize for that." Anne stood up and went over to her husband's side.

"Besides, I am your true wife and queen now, and I have a little surprise for you." Henry turned to her with

121

a look of desire in his eyes. "I knew it, my young and fertile queen. You are with child again!" Anne blushed with excitement. "Yes, my love, I am, and I have a different feeling about me this time. I am positive that this child will be the son you have prayed for and yearned for so long." Henry kissed her hungrily, pulling her in for better access to her entire body. "Oh Anne, please say that I can have you here, right now. I burn for you. I need to be close to you. You cannot be more than a couple of weeks along, so no harm can come from us celebrating this glorious news." Anne thought for a moment, but quickly lost all train of thought. Henry began to kiss her bare neck, unclasping her necklace before continuing his descent to her bodice. Anne moaned in surrender, letting Henry continue on his quest. He picked her up and set her down on the bench that sat in front of his bed. After he released her, he proceeded to kiss and fondle her swollen breasts that indicated she was with child. As his mouth lingered there, Anne felt his hands slide up her skirts until they came to rest between her thighs. She was already anxious for him to take her, but Henry had other things in mind.

Before she could catch her breath, Henry was diving under her skirts. Anne felt his hot breath as he kissed her aching loins. She laid back on the bed so that Henry could have full access to her. Her whole body burned with desire. She longed to be naked and entwined with Henry's nakedness, but he had yet not finished what he had set out to do. The sensations he brought out in her made her cry out when she reached the point of ecstasy. Then, just when Anne thought she might faint from her passions, Henry was inside her. He moaned with excitement and pleasure. Anne wrapped her legs around his waist, moving along with his body to further both their ultimate desires. It did not take Henry long to conquer her, and Anne once again felt the heat of pleasure flowing through her body.

"I love you, Anne. More than I have loved anyone else. You are my true match in life and in love." He pulled himself up beside her on the bed, and Anne laid her head on his chest. "I love you, Henry, my beloved." His heart was beating wildly, and without any hesitation, both of them fell asleep. They were brought out of their slumber by Cromwell. Before speaking on the other side of the closed door, he cleared his throat before speaking. "Your Majesties, everyone has arrived for the banquet. Shall I prepare to announce you?"

"Cromwell, we will need a few moments to gather ourselves and we shall be out shortly." Henry called out. "My queen, make haste to your chambers and have your ladies dress you in the yellow damask gown, and I shall match you with the same color tunic and robe. Keep in mind, many will see our choice in color as being disrespectful to the late queen, but if they have been educated as we have, they will know that yellow is Spain's color for mourning. Now go quickly, before I decide to ravish you once more before supper. I will be waiting for you outside the banquet hall, so we can be announced." Anne rose and gathered herself before leaving Henry's rooms. She needed to make sure her bodice, skirts and her hair were not in a distorted state before she left.

February, 1536

Anne looked in her hanging closet and saw the bright yellow gown that had been the talk of scandal only a short while ago. No Spanish yellow today, she thought. Her eyes finally rested on the black silk and damask gown that she was to wear today. How could this be? Henry was too young and healthy to be going to his grave so soon. But it was not a dream, because it was Henry's body she saw lying in state for the past few days so all the nobility could pay their respects to their beloved king.

Anne had requested that Henry be dressed in his coronation clothes. She wanted the people to see their king, still exuding power and authority, even in death. She and Elizabeth would be secretly hidden in an observation box inside St. George's Chapel. She did not want everyone starring at them with sadness or distaste. Anne knew that there were still a lot of Catholics in England, even after the Reformation, but keeping Elizabeth shielded from these traitors for as long as she could was her main interest during Henry's final farewell. A beautiful carriage had been constructed and covered in black velvet, on which Henry's coffin would be placed. It would begin its slow progression to St. George's Chapel in Windsor. As with most royal burials, Henry's funeral procession would make an overnight stop at Syon Park, a former abbey, so that the people could pay their respects and say prayers for the late king's soul.

On the evening that Anne and all of Henry's court made it to Syon Park, those who were closest to the king worked alongside volunteer courtiers in placing Henry's body on a makeshift altar. A beautiful wooden canopy had been built, draped with richly decorated black and gold fabric. Several candelabras had been placed around the king and were to stay lit during the night. The doors to the former abbey were opened once the king was made presentable, and people from all over the kingdom gathered to pay their respects to their beloved ruler. Anne was too exhausted to make an appearance. The ride from Whitehall to Syon had left her in such a state that she refused to expose herself to any more looks of sympathy, and in some cases, scorn. Adding to all the overwhelming events, the pains had returned in her swollen belly.

"Mary, I don't think that I can stand another long night of receiving any more visitors. I must rest for both my health and that of my unborn prince. Please pass on my regards to those who ask about my health." Her sister nodded and helped Anne change from her riding clothes to a more comfortable gown. The rain had turned the air extremely cold and left Anne wishing for warmer weather. She wished more than ever that Henry were alive and not lying in a wooden, velvet covered coffin in the main banqueting hall of the abbey. A sharp sense of pain surged her heart at the thought of him lying there. "How can this be? I'm too young to be a widow, much less a widowed queen. I simply cannot bear the thought of never seeing, hearing, or feeling Henry's presence again. This is not how our lives were supposed to be." A swarm of tears streamed down her face and continued until she had fallen asleep.

Dreams plagued her sleep with all forms of emotions. Three years of marriage had not been long enough for everything that she and Henry had planned during their seven-year courtship, but apparently, it was God's will for Anne to carry on Henry's legacy and uphold every dream he had for his kingdom. Things were never going to be the same, and that's what scared Anne the most. There was an abundance of uncertainty, and not enough solidarity to ease her troubled mind. Life was going to be an adventure, and she intended to proceed in the hopes of continuing the perfect monarchy that Henry had fought so hard to build.

Chapter Eleven

February, 1536

"Your Grace, I'm sorry to disturb you, but we must make ready for the final length of our journey to St. George's. I have prepared you a hot lavender bath to help calm your anxiety." Madge had begun to draw back the drapes to allow the flames from the fireplace illuminate the room. Anne still felt exhausted, and for a brief moment, she wanted to close her eyes once more in hopes that all of this had been nothing but a very bad dream. She could handle any nightmare except this one that she had been forced into living. The ten long years that she and Henry had together had once felt like forever, but now that Henry was truly gone, she would gladly relive all three thousand six hundred and fifty days that made her most happy.

While Anne lay back against the large bathing tub, thoughts seemed to flood her mind and leave just as quickly. Never in her wildest dreams did she think that Henry would die before her. While the king's moods changed quite frequently, she had always thought that if she would be unsuccessful in providing the king with a living male heir that her time as wife and queen would be cut short like Catherine's, or if the unthinkable would happen—if her pregnancy and delivery went wrong. It was not uncommon for women to die during or after child birth, peasants and noblewomen alike. Child bearing was not an easy thing, and while some women could produce and delivery healthy children, there still were many complications that could occur, even with the most skilled midwives. Anne scooped some of the warm water over her swollen belly, thinking back to the day Elizabeth was born.

1533

The seventh of September, 1533, had begun as any normal day. Anne had been in her confinement for a little over two months, patiently awaiting the arrival of her first child. Mary, Nan and Madge had been busy making ready everything that the midwife would need in order to deliver the much-anticipated prince. Henry had visited her often during the past few days, eagerly waiting for any sign that his son would be born. "My dear husband, these things take time. We could be here all night and pray for God to make haste, but I do not believe your son will make his much-anticipated arrival until he is ready."

Anne felt most vulnerable when Henry was not at her bedside. Even though she had been behind closed doors and blocked windows, she could still hear the liveliness of the court, almost every night, coming from the banquet hall. She could hear laughter and clapping as everyone enjoyed themselves at the expense of the king. But there had been only one thing that really troubled her the most: Henry's infidelity. Rumors around the court had begun to circulate that Henry had been captivated by Elizabeth Harvey, a friend and lady of Lady Mary's household. The Spanish ambassador, Eustace Chapuys, had let the information slip in one of his letters to the pope. At first, Anne had been beside herself with grief and anger at how quickly and easily her husband had managed to forget his love for her. The child that thrived eagerly inside her womb had been a constant reminder of just how persuasive Henry could be. Her father had come to visit shortly after her confinement and found Anne lost in deep thought.

"Anne, you look well this evening. But I can sense something is bothering you."

"All is well, Father. The child within me grows by the minute, and I have no doubt that we shall have our much-awaited prince soon. What's new at court? I have missed out on several gatherings and hear only small amounts of gossip, of which I can neither acknowledge nor deny."

"Daughter, I know that you are in a fragile state and not used to being kept away from socializing, but everyone is eagerly awaiting the arrival of the prince."

"Father, please do not play coy with me. I am no fool. My ladies tell me that the king has taken a mistress to his bed since I came into my confinement. I know the king still loves me above all others, and with this miracle I am about to give to him, he will hold me higher still, but I do not see why he must take to his bed any woman that catches his eye, especially when he knows how upset it makes me." Anne had looked over at her window to avoid her father's concerned gaze. "You see, Anne, it is not an uncommon thing for a man to seek pleasures elsewhere while his wife is great with child. For His Majesty, it is expected of him, since it is for the sake and well-being of you, his queen, and his unborn child. You must not take to heart these small indiscretions, but be dismissive of them, for when you have safely delivered your son, no other woman will be able to hold a candle to how high His Majesty will place you."

She had known that her father was trying to ease her agitation with the notion of another woman in her marital bed, but no matter how gently and justifiably he tried, Anne could not see past her natural instinct to be jealous.

Around two in the afternoon, the first signs of labor began. Anne had been sleeping, when a sharp pain went through her belly and radiated to her back. When she called out for her sister, she felt the need to stand up and when she did, her water broke almost instantly. The pain intensified dramatically. The midwife was sent for, and a message was delivered to the king that his son was ready to make his appearance. While Anne had been in confinement, Henry had been planning a most elaborate event of celebrations that spared no expense. He had planned grand banquets with all the finest foods and wines to be given to anyone close enough to receive them. Several large cannons would be lit and fired in honor of his son and heir as well as for his most beloved queen. When the king was told that Anne's labor had begun, he immediately summoned the kitchens to begin the meal preparations. He went directly to his chambers to change into his finest robes, in which he would soon hold his much-awaited newborn son.

"Push, Your Majesty, that's it. Not much longer now, you're doing perfectly well for your first delivery," the midwife encouraged Anne. "For the love of all the saints, how do women commit to doing this more than once?" Anne said between her contractions. "I feel like my entire being is trying to come out with the arrival of the prince." A few of the ladies had laughed softly, hoping to lighten the atmosphere.

"Mary, how in God's name did you manage this? I feel like I might die from the pain."

"Sweet sister, it is all worth it when you see your baby. This I can promise you."

Another sharp pain radiated through Anne's body, and Mary and Nan each grabbed one of Anne's legs in order to help with the final moments of labor. "One more push, Your Grace, and you can meet your son." With one final effort, Anne clinched her teeth, bearing down as hard as she could to push out the child that she had been carrying for nine long months. The very second that she felt like she could do no more, a rush of relief came over her, and through her panted breaths, the sweet sound of her baby's cry filled the room. Anne smiled that her son was finally and safely delivered.

"Hand him to me, please. I must see my sweet son." Anne held out her arms to receive her newborn baby, the true Prince of England. *Oh, how Henry would be so happy and grateful for everything I have been through this day.* Her sister wiped Anne's face with a cool wet cloth to clear her of the sweat of giving birth. "Mary, is something wrong? Why has my son not been given to me yet?"

Her sister seemed a little hesitant in answering, but managed to keep her emotions to herself. Within a few moments, Mary had gone over to where the midwife was washing and wrapping the crying baby in a swaddling blanket. Mary took the tiny baby from the midwife, who resumed her duties in making sure the afterbirth was delivered. As the room remained quiet, Mary came to Anne's bedside. "Your Majesty, I humbly congratulate you on the safe and healthy delivery of a most beautiful daughter."

A daughter, a baby girl, no, this cannot be. I was supposed to have a son, a prince that is the perfect image of his father. "A baby girl? No, this cannot be. Check again, I promised Henry a son not a daughter." Anne felt all the blood rush from her head, and the room seemed to fade away as the tiny baby was placed in her waiting arms. The child was not the son Henry had entrusted her with having, but was a beautiful little girl instead.

Even though she knew Henry was impatiently awaiting the news of her delivery, Anne asked for the announcement to be postponed for a little while. Mary was true to her word in that all the physical pains from giving birth faded almost completely into the past the very moment Anne had looked into her daughter's blue eyes. But the reality of how well Henry would take the news of her failure was so frightening that she just wanted a few minutes to admire her beautiful daughter before composing herself to receive the king.

Naming her daughter Elizabeth after Henry's late mother was done for a purpose. Perhaps by keeping his mother's name present might help to soften the news. But when Henry could not stand the wait any longer, he insisted that he be let in to see his queen and child.

Cromwell was the one to break the news to Henry that there had been a princess born to the queen, not a prince, as he had hoped. Henry entered Anne's bedchambers with a look of disappointment and betrayal, but he concealed his deepest discontentedness for Anne's failure by bowing to his wife and asking to hold his newborn child.

"She is beautiful like her mother, is she not? Have no fear, my queen, we are both young and healthy. Sons will come; of that, I am certain." After a short visit and an even quicker kiss on Anne's forehead, Henry once again bowed before leaving.

February, 1536

After getting out of the soothing bath, Anne was dried off and dressed in the unwanted black mourning gown. Whether it was the shock of what she was about to do or the persuasion of her displacement, she soon realized that she was fully dressed and ready to see her husband for the very last time. With Mary by her side and the rest of her ladies following closely behind her, Anne made her way to St. George's to pay her final respects to the deceased King of England.

Anne walked within the halls of a hidden passageway that led to the observation box where her six-month old daughter, Elizabeth sat quietly on her wet nurse's lap. Tears formed in Anne's eyes as she gazed upon her sweet daughter's face. Poor angel, she'll never know how much her father grew to love her so. A cushioned chair waited for her to sit down. As she tucked her skirts under her, Anne glanced down to where Henry's preserved body lay in a silent and permanent sleep. She blinked several times to clear her view from the abundance of tears that were falling down her face. The chapel was completely packed with people from all walks of life, peasant and nobleman alike. Normally, the room would be filled with whispers and the mindless chatter of a congregation, waiting for the sermon to begin. But today, the silence was absolutely deafening.

Anne wanted to scream, and her grief consumed her so much that she no longer felt the pains that continued in her stomach. It was not long before the priests and cardinals began the services, conducted in Latin per Henry's request. Anne knew Latin, but for some reason her studies seemed to fail her today. All she could do was stare down at her beloved king and husband secretly wishing he would rise up and walk out, but he did not.

The service seemed to last for hours with no apparent end in sight. Elizabeth had fallen asleep shortly after the ceremony began, and Anne was grateful for that. She, too, wished for peaceful sleep to consume her. Anything to make this day go away. She was brought back into reality when the altar boys began to sing a beautiful piece composed by Thomas Tallis, and Archbishop Cranmer finalized the service with a blessing in Latin.

Anne requested that she and Elizabeth have a few moments alone with Henry before he was placed inside his monument within the chapel walls. Henry's Privy Council ushered the multitude of people out of the chapel as quickly as they could while Anne, Elizabeth, and her ladies made their way to Henry's side. Even in death, Henry looked ever more the strong and handsome king that he had been merely a month ago. It was almost too much to bear. Anne knelt down beside her husband and took one of his hands in hers. She held it close to her heart and let her tears fall upon his cold skin. "Oh my darling, sweet husband, my heart is broken. Your son is the only one who can feel the true extent of my sorrow. I mourn for him as I do you, because he will never meet you this side of Heaven. Your Elizabeth sleeps soundly and does not understand that she will never see your face again. For her, I hope you passed on your ability to protect England until your son takes the throne. I only hope that she finds a husband worthy of her love and status. Being a daughter of the strongest king in all of Europe, it will be hard to find a man as worthy as you. But *I* will miss you most of all. There is a hole in my soul that cannot be patched or replaced. I make this last promise to you. I will guide our children in the right direction befitting both a prince and princess. You will always be with me, everywhere I go, and I hope to make you proud, my most loving husband and king. This I do swear to you in front of God and all his angels."

With her final words and a last kiss placed upon his lips, Anne stood up and curtsied to her husband and king for the last time, leaving him with her motto, *"I will forever remain the most happy."*

STEPHANIE BASCO SULLIVAN

Chapter Twelve

With the loss of one life
There comes another.
Sometimes it's welcomed
Like a sister or brother.
Even through death
Our lives must go on;
There are those who stay with us
And can be replaced by none.

February, 1536

Anne made it through her husband's departure as bravely as she could. And those around her were in awe at how their queen remained firmly grounded with everything that needed to be done. But behind closed doors, in the privacy of her chambers, Anne wept for her absent husband. It had been two weeks since Henry had been interred within his final resting place. Holbein had been commissioned to make a beautiful marble plaque to mark the great king's effigy. The Privy Council had wanted a grand display to be erected to represent their beloved king, but Anne had managed to have one last say in how her husband would be remembered.

"My Lords, I know that my husband and king was a very great man and deserved the best memorial to represent his life, but does it not make better sense to, just for now, save as much money for any possible and unplanned attacks that may try to take over what Henry worked so hard for? There have been some reports that the Lady Mary has managed to secure herself a small army while she is in exile, waiting until she is able to challenge the validity of my daughter's legal and binding right to her father's throne?"

"Your Grace, the Act of Succession that the late king had put into place shortly after Princess Elizabeth's birth does hold credence within the realm, but I'm afraid that while the Lady Mary is no longer legally recognized as an heir to her late father's throne, there still remains the Catholic Church and the conflict with His Holiness, the Pope." Cromwell wanted Anne to be reminded that even though Henry was declared Supreme Head of the Church of England, with his untimely death, there were some things that could not be overlooked.

"I see, Lord Cromwell. I wonder, how do the rest of you feel regarding the disinherited Mary? And please, do not be discrete because of my sex. I still carry within my belly another child that has yet made his way into this world and if he is the prince that Henry so desired, then no one, not even the pope, can dispute my son's claim to his late father's throne."

Anne looked around the room at each member of the Council, hoping that someone would be brazen enough to explain what she must be unaware of. Finally, a familiar face sat forward in his chair, and after a deep breath, began to speak.

"Your Majesty, I have it on good authority that the Lady Mary has had full communications with His Holiness within days of learning of her father's death. With the small amount of what remained of her late mother's dowry, Lady Mary has been able to secure her safety here in England with the protection of those who still practice the Catholic faith. The Spanish ambassadors have been to Rome a few times in hopes of having an audience with the pope, but so far have not succeeded. His Holiness, while not in favor of England remaining a Protestant, nation does not see you as a threat—that is, until you give birth to your child."

"What does it matter when I give birth? How could an infant possibly persuade the decision of the pope to provide protection for a nobody? This kingdom has held its own, with myself as its queen, for nearly four years, and I have no plans to risk the future of my children based on idle gossip from the Lady Mary."

"The fact remains, Your Grace, that whether you have a son or yet another daughter, the majority of this kingdom is, and always will be, devoted to the Catholic faith. The king himself still practiced some of the customs of the Catholic Church, even though he claimed himself head of the Church of England. And while there are many Protestants that live and worship freely, there are those that signed the Oath who never intended to fully displace their Catholic faith behind closed doors. These are the very people that we should be mindful of. They are the ones who have remained loyal to Catherine of Aragon's daughter. To them, Mary has been treated with the deepest disrespect that any natural born princess could ever be treated. They will remain forever resentful towards those who displaced her and her late mother."

Anne knew that every word was true, and she felt the natural instinct to protect her children as well as herself. She looked around the table again. She tried to see through each man's solemn face in hopes that somehow, there would be an answer. "Lord Suffolk, you have remained silent. What do you think of the situation presented before us?" Charles looked at Anne with a blank face. She knew that since Henry's death, the safety and well-being of Elizabeth, her unborn child, and her own person had become something of a chore for him. She had thought that since they had made peace for Henry's sake, while he was still clinging to life, that they had pushed aside their petty and hasty misunderstandings of one another. But before Henry's body had been settled in its final resting place, Charles had resumed his hatred for her.

Was it because he resented her for not being satisfied with being Henry's mistress? Was it because Catherine and her daughter had been set aside when Henry claimed he had sinned against God by marrying his brother's widow? Or was it simply because Henry chose her, a woman of ignoble birth, to be his wife and queen? After all, Charles had been very adamant in trying to persuade Henry that Anne was not suitable to be the Queen of England.

During Henry's faithful pursuit of her, many rumors were spread around court on how Anne had behaved herself while at French court. Of course, her sister Mary's eagerness to find her way into Henry's bed had not helped Anne's reputation. Then the question came about of whether or not Anne had secretly married

Henry Percy, even after they were forbidden to carry on their courtship. Everyone had assumed that Anne had slept with Percy just to spite Henry. Of course, she had not damaged her name or her virtue as many people had presumed. "Idle and jealous gossip, my love" she had reassured Henry.

It did not take much for a woman's reputation to be ruined by the wagging tongues of bored and snooty members of the court.

"Your Grace, I have stood by your side even though I have felt differently than most. I wanted to keep the love of my friend and king. And while I find myself divided between wanting to provide security for all of Henry's children, born and unborn, I cannot help but wonder just how safe you and your position truly are. Many have resented you for things the king did in your name, but I see no need for alarm until your child is delivered. If it is the son and heir that Henry had prayed and sacrificed his kingdom as well as his mortal soul for, then there will be no need for Mary to proclaim war against the crown. But if another daughter is to be presented, I fear that the Lady Mary will see her chance at taking her father's throne as her birth right."

The words stung Anne to her very core, but she knew that Charles was right. Every possible measure needed to be taken in order for her position to remain safe and secure for her children. "My Lords, I humbly ask of you, please place aside any hard feelings you bear me as Henry's wife and queen and think only of his true heirs, the Princess Elizabeth and the child I have yet to deliver. As of now, the Act of Succession will remain in place for my protection and that of my

141

children. If and when the Lady Mary shows any signs that she has intensions of reclaiming her father's throne, then, and only then, will we take action."

Anne was feeling very tired and wanted nothing more than to retire to her rooms and close her eyes for a little while. "My Lords, I must take my leave from today's business. My father, the Earl of Wiltshire, will represent me in my absence." A sharp pain riddled her stomach and made her stand up. All of the Councilmen stood in respect as Anne quickly collected herself.

"Before I take my leave, I want to thank each of you for the kindness you have shown me during these horrible and most trying of times. My beloved king and husband would have just cause to promote you all within your stations. I humbly ask forgiveness for lack of attention to matters of state. You see, I know that most of you were against the king's decision to marry me and discharge his former wife and queen, but I do believe that you all truly loved and cherished your king. I respectfully thank you for standing by his side. even if you disapproved of his choice in me for his companion. I want nothing more than to keep England safe and prosperous for those who will carry on our names after we are gone." She felt a twinge of sadness pass through her heart as she placed her hand on her belly. "I don't know if I carry a prince or another princess. Only time will tell, but I humbly ask that you pray, if not for me, then for Henry's unborn child. It will be difficult enough having this child amongst so many that seek to harm him but even more challenging without the love and protection of my beloved husband."

She bowed her head to show a measure of appreciation and then took her leave. Her father and brother George would make sure to keep her informed of everything that she needed to know. She just needed to rest.

The cool air from the night sky felt good against Anne's cheek as she lay in her bed. She had slept for several hours after leaving the Council. Nothing of great importance must have occurred, because her father had not come. Her stomach let out a howling growl, and suddenly, food was all she could think about. "Nan, has supper come up for me? I am completely and utterly famished." The curtains that divided her rooms had been closed to keep out any noises from her ladies, who had been working on their sewing. Nan appeared with a lit candle in her hand. She glanced over at the dwindling flame in the fireplace and called for more wood to be brought in. "For the love of all the saints, your window is cracked open. No wonder it feels like the ice in here." She raced to the window and quickly closed it.

Nan made her way to the burning embers in Anne's fireplace. With an iron rod, she poked at the angry coals until they stirred back to life. "I'll send for your supper. I was beginning to think that you were going to sleep all night, but I knew that the young babe would wake you soon enough." Nan collected Anne's night cloak and helped her into it before heading to the parlor. "I must have great timing," Anne said as her door opened, and several trays of food and drink were brought in and placed on her table. As she sat down and placed a cloth in her lap, she looked around at her ladies. Each one had managed to find something

143

constructive to do. But Anne did not want to eat alone. She was used to being dressed and joining Henry in the dining hall or his chambers to eat, but that would no longer happen.

"Ladies, please join me. There is more food here than I can possibly eat, even if I'm eating for two and I could use some friendly or idle gossip. There's no need for formalities tonight. I'm simply Anne, and we are all friends." Her ladies looked puzzled and confused at her request, but slowly, each one gathered around Anne's small table and waited for their gracious host to fill her plate first before taking of their own. Conversation was, at first, very slow to start, but after a few glasses of wine and several laughs, everything seemed to fall into place. For once, Anne did not feel completely alone.

Chapter Thirteen

May, 1533

"Why does he hate me so much? He called me a little girl in front of everyone. I have been humiliated and offended, as I should be." Anne was trying to stay calm and collected, but Cardinal Woolsey had crossed the line with his rude and arrogant behavior. Did he not value his position, or was he simply stupid? "Henry, did you hear what I said? He speaks to me as if I were a commoner or just another fling of yours." She had waited patiently for Henry's reply. "After all, you did send for me, did you not?"

"Anne, my own heart, please don't let Woolsey spoil my surprise. It's very hard to keep some things to myself, and you, my darling, are one of those things. I will speak to him later, but for now, there is another matter at hand." Henry rose from his chair and walked over to her. He smelt like wine and bread. She loved the way he smelled. He put his arms around her small waist and pulled her in. He bent down and properly greeted her with a passionate kiss. He had always known how to distract her every time she wanted to discuss anything of importance.

After a few moments of a very heated kiss, Anne pulled away from his embrace, casually walking around him. He let her hand slide down his shirt, grazing ever so lightly across his doublet. She could tell that he was already mad with desire but she was not ready to give in so quickly. "You said that you have a surprise for me did you not?" She asked seductively. Henry came up behind her and pulled her as close to him as he could. She could feel his hunger for her through her skirts while he leaned in closer. "Archbishop Cranmer has declared the annulment of my marriage to Catherine," he said in a low voice. His hot breath caressed the back of her neck and sent chills of desire throughout her body. "Did you hear what I said, my love? Declared an annulment; do you know what that means? Mary is no longer my heir, and you are the legitimate Queen of England."

Anne turned around and met his gaze. "Can it be true? Oh, Henry, how long have I waited for this moment. I had almost given up hope of ever being able to openly call myself your wife. Does this mean that I can begin to plan our public wedding?" Henry's face went from a proud smile to a somber one.

"My dear Anne, we have already had a ceremony, albeit a small one. Besides, I have been planning your coronation for a few weeks now, and that, my love, will serve well as our wedding day. I have no doubt that the people of England will love and admire my new wife and queen, but I do not wish to flaunt my happiness in their faces while the loss of their former queen commences. I want them to fall in love with you just as I have, not consider you an enemy."

"An enemy, why would they think that of me? I have shown them no cause to dislike me." She could feel a hint of anger piercing through her body.

"My sweet, sweet Anne, I know that you have not personally given them reason to be angry, but as you know, I have had to do some very displeasing things in order to make you recognized as my queen. I am breaking with the Catholic Church, and in their eyes, I have been abandoned by God in doing so. Catherine was not just a queen; she was a very loving and giving queen when it came to the people. To them, I have not only refused to settle this delicate matter in Rome, I have removed Catherine from this place along with my only daughter and, in many eyes, the rightful heir to the throne. I have displaced them to the farthest corners of England. And the people are not so easy to convince without the blessing from the pope. Change is something they do not take kindly to."

Anne knew that he was right. But why should she have to suffer in silence when she had done nothing wrong? Surely, she had made some enemies at court, but most of them were of Catherine's household. Now that they no longer resided in the palace, she had thought herself somewhat freed from scandal and harsh rumors. She had been so careful not to allow Henry carnal knowledge of her before they had married, for fear that he might speak of it to his best friend and confidant, the Duke of Suffolk, Charles Brandon.

"I understand, my love. I want to be your loving wife in every way. Respected and loved, just as your brother's wife had been to you for all these years. I only wanted to show my love for you through the public exchanging of our wedding vows."

But Henry could not be swayed. Their secret marriage had become widely known, and he felt his only step forward was the coronation, especially since Anne was already with child.

Henry kept to his word, and after a few days, the very prideful Cardinal Woolsey sent to her a beautiful pearl broach and a formal invitation for her and the king to dine with him on an evening of their choosing. Henry and Anne accepted the invitation, and Anne intended to wear one of her nicest gowns, planning to showcase the beautiful broach that Woolsey had sent to her. She asked Henry to be present during this most important gown selection. She wanted them to wear the same colors so that everyone, including Cardinal Woolsey, could see just how in love they were.

"What about this one?" Anne pulled out a deep green gown that had silver beading throughout. "No, I like that gown, but not for this occasion. What about something in blue?" Anne turned back to her gowns and began looking through them for anything blue. But she came up wanting. "I don't have anything in blue, I'm afraid. There's no time to have one made. Is there another color that you would prefer?" She asked with a look of frustration. Henry snapped his fingers, and a young woman brought in a box tied with a blue silk ribbon. "I think that this will be the gown you will wear, and I have just the robes to match it perfectly."

She walked over to the table where Henry was sitting, and after the young woman left, Anne quickly untied the ribbon, lifting the lid off the box. Inside lay the most beautiful, bright, royal blue gown she had ever seen. The bodice was made of a velvet and silk damask fabric that had tiny sapphires and pearls sewn into the trim. "Oh Henry, how beautiful!" She continued to pull the gown out of the box, laying it across her bed. The front panel of the skirt had very intricate needlework, with two blue birds sewn into the fabric. It was truly a sight to behold, and she had known that with this gown, everyone would know just how much Henry loved her.

She knelt down beside him and kissed him eagerly. Henry pulled her up into his lap and wrapped his long arms around her. He began to kiss her neck and wanted to proceed further, but Anne quickly pulled away. She slid her hands down his chest and slowly climbed out of his lap. While she kept her eyes on him, she let her hands provide him with a much desired *thank you*.

February, 1536

A loud clap of thunder woke Anne from her sleep. The sun had not risen yet, but the lightning was so bright that it lit up her room like the sun. Seconds later, a very loud clap of thunder rolled across the sky and seemed to resonate in her ears. Madge was sleeping on the cot next to her bed and did not seem to notice the loud storm that was forming outside. Just as another flicker of lightning crossed the sky, a hard and sharp pain seared through her body but this time the pain did not stop.

"Madge, wake up. I need you to help me. I have the worst pains I have ever felt, and I may need the midwife." While Anne started pulling back her covers, Madge called out to Nan, who was sleeping in the parlor. While Nan rushed to light some candles so they could see, Anne finally managed to free herself from her blankets. Nan brought a candle over to the bedside and proceeded to check for any signs of labor. "Oh, good Lord, Madge, fetch the midwife quickly!" Nan did not have to say anything. Anne had already figured out what was happening. She had felt the blood while removing the blankets. She was losing her baby. She was into her fifth month, but no child had ever survived birth so early. "No, dear God, no! Not my baby, please not my sweet baby."

The pain surged through her body again, causing Anne to naturally push. She pressed her knees together to prevent the child from coming out, but the pain was so severe that all she could think about was how to make it stop. Within a few moments and one big push, the tiny babe was delivered. Anne reached down and pulled the lifeless little body into her arms and saw that it was, indeed, her son. The prince that Henry had wanted for so long had finally come to be, but he was not meant to stay. Madge arrived with the midwife and found Anne cradling her stillborn son in her arms. There was absolutely nothing to be done. All the hopes and dreams that Anne had envisioned for this moment now lay soundly behind her son's closed eyes.

"I'm so sorry, Your Majesty. I came as quickly as I could. Are there no signs of life from the child?" The midwife asked. "No, he was born into God's hands and cradled by his father. There was nothing to be done." Nan took the tiny little newborn from Anne's arms, reassuring her that as soon as she had cleaned him up and swaddled him, she would allow Anne all the time she needed to say her goodbyes. The midwife made the sign of the cross and held fast to the golden cross necklace around her neck. Anne still needed to be tended to in order to make sure she delivered the afterbirth that had surrounded the tiny prince. Once Anne had been tended to and no more bleeding from her miscarriage was present, the bed linens had been stripped and remade in order for Anne to resume her position in bed.

Within half an hour, Anne gave birth to her much-desired son, washed off, dressed in warm gowns and helped back into bed to receive her sweet, lifeless baby boy.

Mary was the one who brought the bathed and swaddled child to her sister's bedside. Anne found herself torn between holding her departed son or merely requesting that he be made ready for his funeral. She felt so exhausted and broken-hearted that, once again, she had failed Henry, even in death. But she could not fight the instinct to see her son that would now join his father. Mary handed the little prince to his mother. Outwardly, he looked perfectly normal. His head was full of the bright red hair that he had obviously inherited from his father. Anne began to unfold the cloth that had been carefully swaddled around her baby. Ten fingers, ten toes with a soft pout to his lips. He was so perfect, and Anne could have sworn that he was just sleeping, but he was not. "I wish to call him Harry in honor of his father, the King of England. He is every bit his father's image, and now, Henry has his much-desired son."

The pain of yet another loss consumed Anne. All she could do was hug her precious son and say her final farewell to the very thing she had prayed for, for so long, a son and heir. "Mary, please send for my father, and once he has left me, send for Master Cromwell. This will change a lot of things that the Privy Council had placed their hopes on and I need to announce this misfortune as softly as I can." Mary wiped away the tears that she had shed for the departed child and slightly curtsied to her sister to pay her respects. Anne's father and brother George entered into her bedchambers soon thereafter. Both went down on bended knee before going over to see the child, gently swaddled in his mother's loving arms.

Setting aside her grief, Anne knew what must be done. "Before you say your peace," she told them, "know that I have done nothing to dislodge this child from my womb. God has chosen for this precious baby to join his father in the arms of Heaven. Elizabeth is to be moved within my household for added security. We have lost our prince, and when word reaches the Lady Mary, the tides are likely to shift. We must, at all cost, show no weakness in our loss. Cry if you must, but do so behind closed doors for there are many enemies at court that wait for the weak to be singled out. Please don't shed your tears in this room. A prince has been born and died. Arrangements will be made for his final farewell, now please leave me to grieve my son."

After about an hour, Cromwell entered into Anne's chambers with his hat in his hand. He was announced as he entered Anne's bedchamber, where she was still holding her departed son. Cromwell bowed in a graceful manner, wanting to keep the atmosphere as somber as possible. "Your Majesty, I am regretfully sorry. I, too, have lost loved ones that left this world sooner than their time." Thomas wiped a stray tear from his cheek before rising to his feet. "Please, Thomas, come see my son, Henry's son. And if it's not too painful, you can share with me of those whom you have lost." Cromwell walked slowly to Anne's bedside and glanced down at the unmoving babe in Anne's arms.

"He's perfect, Your Grace, the image of his late father." Anne motioned for him to sit in the chair beside her bed, where just over five months ago, Henry had sat and doted on his daughter, Elizabeth. "Thomas, of whom do you speak that you have lost?" With a small hesitation, Thomas seemed to travel back to a different time and place. "I had a wife, Elizabeth, who gave me four beautiful children. A son, Gregory, and three daughters, Anne, Grace, and Jane. While my son is still alive and well, my poor wife and daughters died after they succumbed to the sweating sickness in 1529. I dare say that those were the darkest days of my entire existence."

Anne had not known of Thomas's losses, and she felt tears gathering in her eyes in sympathy. "Thomas, I had no idea of your losses. I am most saddened at the burden you have carried for seven years."

"Your Grace, I have come to realize that we are only here for a short time, though for some of us it feels like a full lifetime. How we live our lives while we are on this Earth only gives us time to prepare our souls for our final and lasting destination. Just as you, I, too, shall see my wife and girls once God calls me home."

His words comforted her yet left her yearning for the day in which she, too, would rejoin Henry, her stillborn daughter, and now, her beloved son.

The young prince's funeral was a small and intimate affair. Anne had made it abundantly clear that she did not want the people of England to crowd the halls of Whitehall as they had when Henry had been laid to rest only last month. Only Anne, her ladies, her father, brother, and the members of the Privy Council were allowed to attend. The tiny prince was placed in a small white coffin with the name Harry Rex inscribed on the top. A Protestant ceremony took place, followed by a Catholic mass. It was decided that her son be laid to rest alongside his father. Who better to look after him than his own father?

Anne did allow a messenger to announce the prince's death, followed by one cannon to be fired, signifying that a member of the royal household had died. It did not seem real. The cannon fire should have signified the birth of a healthy son and heir of Henry VIII. Instead, the sound of the blast, which echoed through the sky for miles, reminded Anne that not only was her husband and king dead, so, too, was her son. At that very moment, she had never felt so alone, nor so vulnerable. Had her sweet son lived, her position, as well as Elizabeth's, would have been safe and secure from all of Europe. But by now, the news of the prince's death was bound to have reached the outer realms of the kingdom and beyond, playing right into the Lady Mary's awaiting hands. Now nothing, or no one, was safe from rebellions that could find their way into Anne's court.

Chapter Fourteen

1549

The years have remained in quiet slumber with some bouts of somberness. Those I have loved have come and gone like the seasons that drape this land as a blanket. My eyes have seen the changes of time, leaving my heart to consume its carnage. With new births, there have always followed death, caring not of age or sex. Some battles have been won while others have been lost never to be spoken of again. The one constant has been my darling Elizabeth. She alone has been my saving grace and sweetest ambition, the very essence of her father, Henry, the Eighth of that name. Through years and hours of prayer and solitude, she has been made ready for what is rightfully hers by birth and she shall become victorious in all things.

In the blink of an eye, Anne found herself sitting in front of her dressing mirror. Age had come gracefully to her, and for that, she was very grateful. She had passed her fortieth year, and only the small lines around the edges of her eyes gave way to her years of living as her daughter's mentor. She had done it; she had managed to keep her daughter alive for nearly fourteen years without much retaliation from the ever-present Lady Mary. It had not been easy, and at times,

Anne and her daughter, now aged sixteen years, often had to find refuge and comfort within the confines of the very churches that Henry had worked to dissolve. Mary, herself, had tried several times to rally troops from Rome and Spain to overthrow Anne and her daughter, but with the help of Archbishop Cranmer, her very ambitious uncle the Duke of Norfolk and other members of the Privy Council had managed to cut Mary's advancements before any serious claims could be made. Even though most of Henry's England had returned to the Catholic faith, there were still enough devoted Protestants left to help secure Elizabeth's claim to the throne.

Anne knew that not everyone was satisfied with a Protestant queen taking the great king's throne, but no one dared to openly question it, either. Life for Anne had not been a smooth one. Her father, Thomas Boleyn, the Earl of Wiltshire, had fallen sick only three years after Henry's own death, and after a brief illness, had succumbed to his fever. While Anne had loved her father, she had also found fault with him. He had been so quick to side with her uncle in securing the Boleyns' rise to power by using his daughters' virtues and reputations in order to achieve it.

Anne had watched her poor sister, Mary, become the scandal of Queen Catherine's court, losing her husband as well as a chance at a normal life outside Anne's court, but sadly, Anne had needed her sister close by her when life at court had begun to change. Looking back at everything she and her sister had gone through made Anne feel sorry that she had relied on Mary's council during the darkest days of her marriage to the very man who had made Mary his mistress. Now, even

Mary was gone. She had fallen ill, and while physicians had bled her and expected a full recovery, Mary had died in 1540 at only forty years of age. Of course, Anne had made sure her sister's children were well cared for and protected. The day of Mary's funeral, Anne was beside herself with grief. She had stayed in bed until everyone had left the feast, prepared in Mary's honor, before she dressed and went to the crypt where her sister had been laid to rest.

Anne had found some friendship in Thomas Cromwell until he had undermined Elizabeth's tutors, as he, himself, had felt led support Mary's claim to the throne. After sending him to the Tower, Anne had confronted him in a discussion that would change both their lives.

1540

"My Lord Cromwell, why, after all these years have you betrayed me? Is it not enough that I have stood by your side on many matters regarding the concerns and the welfare of this kingdom? I considered you a trusted friend. What has changed?"

"Your Grace, my words, I fear, only fall on deaf ears. The number of supporters for the Lady Mary have climbed into multitudes, and I fear that the Princess Elizabeth will not have the much-needed support of the English people. I do not question her claim, but with all due respect, Henry's marriage to you was not seen valid nor recognized in the eyes of the Catholic Church and across the majority of Europe. When Queen Catherine died, I recall that you both donned yellow garments after hearing of her passing and the English people, who adored her, very much took it as an insult."

"If you were a well-informed man as most are at court, you would have realized that yellow is the color of mourning in Spain. No underlying meaning was portrayed, except by those who already held me responsible for her dismissal. You know as I do, Henry was not easily swayed from something he wanted. How he stayed in love with me for seven years without me going to his bed, I will never know."

"Regardless, the times are coming to a head, and only one daughter of the late king will occupy his vacant throne. While Elizabeth is only nine years from assuming that role, the Lady Mary is twenty-four years old and of proper age. There has been talk about her marriage to Spain to secure her father's throne. I firmly stand with which ever head the crown is placed upon regardless of my true feelings. I have my family to think of, or what's left of it."

"I'm heartbroken, dear Thomas, and I have no words to ease your tormented conscience. But my daughter's claim is worth fighting for, and if you cannot see her as your one true queen when the time comes, I cannot guarantee your safety, or your life."

That was the last time Anne ever saw Cromwell alive. The Privy Council thought it best to cleanse the court of anyone who may be deemed a threat to Elizabeth's throne, even if that meant capturing the Lady Mary herself and securing her in the tower. Cromwell was taken to Tower Hill on the twenty-eighth of July, 1540, and was beheaded for committing high treason.

1550

Cromwell's words had rung true after the years of his execution. While Mary stayed as far from Anne's reach as she could, nothing, not even Mary herself, could have stopped every uprising gathered in her namesake. Before Anne realized it, another season had come and gone. Elizabeth, who was now of age to assume the role her mother had so diligently managed to keep safe for all these years, had decided to throw her mother a birthday feast. There were younger faces at court, consisting of the children who came from the same noble families that had severed ties with her father and mother, yet there still remained a few elders who had managed to cheat death in order to see Elizabeth crowned.

"My Lady Mother, are you ready for your birthday celebrations? Everyone is eagerly awaiting your presence." Anne saw her daughter standing behind her with a giddy smile upon her face. "I see you wore my royal blue gown. It becomes you, my sweet. Your father would be so proud of you and the strong woman you have become. Here, I want to give you a gift."

Anne reached inside her jewelry box and pulled out the pearl broach that Cardinal Woolsey had given to her so many years before. After she pinned it to the bodice of Elizabeth's gown, Anne stood back in admiration. "You truly are a vision to behold."

"Come Mother, make haste. We would not want to keep everyone waiting too long to celebrate the greatest queen ever to grace England's throne." The greatest queen, once maybe, but the years had found themselves hidden within Anne's heart, and she knew that one day, she too, would have to leave her golden daughter to rule and find her own way in this uneven world. After taking one last glance into her mirror, she reached for her daughter's waiting arm and the two Boleyn women walked together as they had done for all these years.

Elizabeth, the First of that name, was crowned in 1550 after turning seventeen years of age. Anne sat near the altar, watching her young daughter walk the very same aisle that she had walked seventeen years ago. Her heart was filled with an enormous amount of pride and accomplishment that her daughter, the little red headed baby girl who had been foretold to be the *son* and heir that Henry had so desperately wanted, was now being crowned and anointed with the same pomp and circumstance as her mother had. No parent could have been more honored than Anne was feeling now. But her celebrations would be short-lived. Anne became ill with a fever a few months into her daughter's reign. The physicians were baffled as to what exactly plagued their former queen, and any newfound treatments were refused by Anne.

"My Lady Mother, please let us try something. There are many new advancements in medicine, and I can have every known physician here within a few days." Elizabeth sat at her mother's bedside while she dipped a linen cloth into a cool bowl of water to wipe her mother's face and neck. "I still need you, now more than ever. Not everyone seems content with having another Protestant queen on the throne of England. Robert Dudley is my only true friend and supporter other than you, but I still feel eyes upon me everywhere

I go, and I hear idle rumors roaming the halls. I still need your guidance in all matters. I truly do not know how you managed this position when you were crowned."

Anne studied her daughter's slender face. Elizabeth may have had her father's beautiful red hair, but Anne also saw herself in her daughter's dark eyes. "You are the daughter of King Henry the VIII and Queen Anne Boleyn. Strength flows through your veins and the force of fire is in your eyes. This is what you were born for. You were the missing piece that I needed in order to fulfill your father's legacy. Countries and their rulers will hear you when you speak, leaving no room for doubt, of this I am certain." Anne reached for a cup of water on her bedside table. "Do not let the idle talk of learned men deter what God has called you to do."

"But mother, what about my half-sister, Mary, she has ten times the support that I could ever dream of having. I fear even the men of my Privy Chamber have found ways of serving both me to my face and Mary behind closed doors. I cannot compete with the Catholic rebellion that has been rumored to support Mary and plan to overthrow my place once you are gone." Anne knew, all too well, the strain and fear her daughter was facing. She reached for Elizabeth's hand and squeezed it gently. "It took seven long and trying years for your father to finally see that kings and queens are anointed by God and not the Catholic Church. My journey to becoming a queen was not an easy one, and I made many enemies, both here and abroad. The English people were not in favor of me replacing Catherine of Aragon as queen. What made it even harder was that I had to serve in her household even before your father chose me to pursue. I was ridiculed and despised everywhere I went, even when your father was finally granted the annulment of his marriage to Catherine. Even after Catherine's death, I was blamed for her early demise, and threats on my life were made." She took another sip of water and repositioned herself to a more comfortable sitting position.

"My darling girl, you are the rightful Queen of England. Trust in that fact, and nothing shall sway you in your plight. Now, I feel I must rest for a little while. You, yourself, should do the same. Age comes quickly upon those who worry too much." Anne closed her eyes, and Elizabeth kissed her mother on her forehead before leaving her mother's chambers.

On her slow walk back to her own chambers, thoughts of her Catholic sister to pursue her. Elizabeth had been given the best education that a princess could have. She was well versed in different languages, the playing of instruments, dancing, and even the art of war. Anne had wanted Elizabeth to be well educated for any type of circumstances should anything should happen to her, and her daughter be left alone. While the Duke of Suffolk, Charles Brandon had not always cared for Anne, but he did care deeply for his best friend's children. He had asked to be one of Elizabeth's tutors and confidants while she was being prepared for her role as queen. The duke had found the princess a delightful child and very much her father's daughter. The two had become practically inseparable until his death in 1545. Elizabeth had gone into a lengthy mourning for her beloved friend and mentor.

Entering her rooms, Elizabeth was greeted by Robert Dudley. He was handsome and kind. Many a night, he had lent his shoulder for her to lean upon. When her mother was fast asleep and the court had dwindled down to what remained of the straggling drunks, Robert would accompany Elizabeth to her chambers. They would stay up the remainder of the night talking about how the two of them would rule England together when the time came. "I would make a very handsome and mysterious king consort, would I not, My Lady?" Elizabeth would giggle with delight and curtsey in front of him as if she were a lady of the court being presented to him. And while they both knew that they could never be married once Elizabeth was crowned, they saw no harm in pretending. Some nights, their harmless acts of diplomacy would take hold of their natural attraction to one another.

Elizabeth had always found Robert very attractive, and when they danced together at court, she could tell he felt fondly of her, as well. Anne had been very steadfast on the importance of Elizabeth keeping her virginity intact until her husband had been chosen for her. But the curiosity between the two young friends soon developed into a deep love for one another. "Robert, how did you get in here?" Elizabeth asked sarcastically. She knew that it did not take much to persuade her ladies to leave her rooms unattended. "Oh, my lady, my queen, you look absolutely delightful tonight. You have bewitched me mind, body, and soul." He moved closer to her as she removed her robes, revealing a pale yellow gown that had a sheer overlay. Before she realized just how close Robert had come up behind her, she felt his soft and gentle kiss on the side of her neck. "My Lord Dudley, do you not know that you need permission from the queen to touch her?" She leaned her head over more so that he had more room to kiss her. "My beautiful queen, may I have the honor of bestowing you with a kiss from your most humble servant?" Elizabeth giggled in agreement and turned to face her handsome caller. The longing for him must have been felt by both, because Robert scooped Elizabeth into his arms and carried her to her open bed. The voice of her mother echoed inside her head telling her to stop, but before she could make reason with her conscience, the two young lovers were quickly removing the pieces of clothing that kept them separated, and while both knew that nothing good could come from this, they wanted this one night together, no matter the repercussions they might face.

In two days' time, Anne's condition had worsened. News of her ill health traveled, and everyone was kept on high alert for any possible invasions. Mary had been spotted only two days' ride from Whitehall Palace. Elizabeth knew that her half-sister had not only heard of Anne's impending death, but that all her Protestant followers were gathering their belongings and closing their stately homes in fear of a Catholic uprising. Elizabeth had remained at her mother's bedside for the past few days, making sure she wanted for nothing. "Elizabeth, this is something I wrote to you not so very long ago. Please read it after I am gone, but please do not cry for me. I have lived a wonderful and exciting life and that is what I will carry with me when I meet my maker. But please do one last thing for me, have only the persons you trust the most to get you to a safe place. Mary will, no doubt, take her place as queen, and

I would not rest easy after this life if something were to happen to you. Be not afraid, for you are both a Tudor and a Boleyn. Do as the Lord commands you, and concede to Mary's wishes in order to survive. She is much older than you and has not yet married. Her bitterness has sealed her fate long before her time. And when that time does come, show your goodness and love in hopes of being crowned, yet again, Queen of England."

When the dawn of another day peered through Anne's windows, her ladies found her in eternal slumber. Elizabeth had vowed to keep all her promises—except one. Before her mother's body was taken to the Chapel of St. Peters, Elizabeth wept for the mother that had not only sacrificed her reputation, but changed the whole of England to secure her daughter's place on the throne of Henry VIII. When Robert had gotten Elizabeth to a safe place after her mother's interment, reports of Mary and eight hundred of her supporters had virtually ridden into England, where Mary was then crowned Queen of England.

Elizabeth still had the one final gift that her mother had left behind, and so she read her mother's last words.

My darling Elizabeth,

From the very moment of your birth, I knew that the stars were in your favor. A princess you were born, but a queen is what you were meant to be. In every way, I have instilled in you the knowledge and virtues worthy of a true queen. Your father passed on his legacy for you to convey to your children, and my darling, you are everything, and much more, than I could have ever asked for. You are my greatest gift, and all my love resides with you. I will soon join your father in God's sweet embrace, but I will forever watch over you. Always be kind, steadfast, and fair to those who come to be your subjects, for they are the ones that will keep your rule everlasting. I beseech you in all things, rule through your faith and protect your values, as I have tried so hard to do all these years. Always know that I will be with you, my golden child. Face your enemies with strength and wisdom, for I know God has blessed you beyond all measure. Look to the sky beyond the clouds, and you shall find me smiling through the sun. And should fate turn with the tides, be smart and resourceful in the wisdom that I have provided you. And always strive to be a fair and just ruler worthy of the crown you have been given. It is—and forever will be—a crown worth fighting for.

Written by the hand of "The Most Happy" queen and your loving mother,

Anne Boleyn

Chapter Fifteen

O n the first of October 1555, Mary Tudor, also known as Bloody Mary, was crowned at Westminster Abbey. She was thirty-seven years of age. Her marriage to Prince Phillip of Spain had taken place on the twenty-fifth of July, 1554, only two days after formally meeting her future husband. Mary and Phillip had borne no children, and Mary's rule became one of turmoil and chaos. On her death bed, she sent for Elizabeth, hoping that she would conform to the Catholic religion. After Elizabeth reassured her sister that she would be a fair and just ruler allowing the people to have the freedom to choose how they worshiped, Mary reluctantly named her half-sister soul heir to their father's throne. Mary died on the seventeenth of November, 1558, at age forty-two, leaving the redheaded daughter that Henry was so disappointed in to resume her place as Queen of England. It was not the son and heir that Henry had very much prayed for, but his second daughter that ruled England for forty-five years in what has been forever called the golden age.

A Crown Worth Fighting For

STEPHANIE BASCO SULLIVAN

References

www.TheAnneBoleynFiles.com

www.TheTudorTravelGuide.com

www.OnTheTudorTrail.com

www.Historic-UK.com

www.Historyextra.com

www.brittanica.com

www.History.com

www.RealRoyalty.com

www.EnglishHistory.net

www.ducksters.com

www.ingramcontent.com/pod-product-compliance
Lightning Source LLC
Chambersburg PA
CBHW022126170626
46808CB00002B/856